The Corner
of Rife and Pacific

Also by Thomas Savage

The Pass
Lona Hanson
A Bargain with God
Trust in Chariots
The Power of the Dog
The Liar
Daddy's Girl
A Strange God
Midnight Line
I Heard My Sister Speak My Name
Her Side of It
For Mary, with Love

The Corner
of
Rife and Pacific

Thomas Savage

William Morrow and Company, Inc.
New York

Library of Congress Cataloging-in-Publication Data

Savage, Thomas.
  The corner of Rife and Pacific
  I. Title.
PS3569.A83C66   1988   813'.54   88-1793
ISBN 0-688-07092-2

Printed in the United States of America

2 3 4 5 6 7 8 9 10

BOOK DESIGN BY ANNA DEUS

For Martha Underwood Wellington
ISAIAH 25:4

Chapter
1

Grayling, Montana, was incorporated at a small celebration in 1890. The first mayor, a man named Rife, was responsible for the fact that CITY OF GRAYLING was printed in huge letters on the sides of the new sprinkler wagon, a big cask on wheels. An ambitious title for a community of not yet a thousand souls, but it was one to live up to. As for Rife, they named a street after him.

A John Metlen sat on the City Council; John was one of half a dozen young men who'd trailed cattle into the valley in the early eighties. John and several others, including Rife and a clever man named Connard, came from families in California who had struck gold before '59, and silver later on. All wanted the rich, wild hay lands along the Grayling River and the good summer pasture high on the mountain slopes. Half a million acres of it still belonged to fewer than five hundred Shoshone Indians who buried their dead in the sliderock or deep in natural caves guarded by rattlesnakes and scorpions.

John Metlen had not come to Montana entirely by choice. His elder brother, a married man, thought John a fellow who "didn't know the value of a dollar"—not much of a fellow to be, and when John also married, his brother remarked, "There's not room for two women on this ranch."

John's father, a widower, had said—gently—"Your head's in the clouds. You've got to come down to earth."

Other sons have heard this. Coming down to earth meant John must go away, because his father, who knew he had practical knowledge only of livestock and hay and weather, and not much of that, had chosen his brother. Other sons have known this.

"But you'll be pretty well fixed, you know, John," the father said. So all he was losing was his home of thirty years. And he was gaining a new home, his wife and a great self-doubt, because he had not been chosen. He could not speak to Lizzie of these things, because a wife looks to a strong man for support, and not to one who has been sent away.

First John went to Montana to build their house, and Lizzie was sent back to her father, who was glad to have her. She had always interested and amused him, and, a surgeon and a serious man himself, he respected her principles. It was because of this that although he had once pointed out that with two hundred thousand people now in San Francisco she could easily find enough whites to teach, he had put nothing in her path when, the government having opened a few schools, she had gone south to instruct the Tehachapi Indians. It was there she had met and married John Metlen, and see what had come of it.

However, the only thing her father said now was "You will miss the city."

Lizzie said, "I will miss you."

They both knew that they might not meet again. The trip to Montana was long and wretched when not hazardous, the

Northern Pacific Railway projected but not built, and letters months in coming, if they arrived at all. For five dollars the Pony Express would get a half-ounce of your mail from west to east, but not through Grayling, Montana. When you left home, chances were that was that.

Meantime John thought that when a man builds a house, he can't go wrong with stone, which lasts. It takes longer, but he hired a clever German stonemason and half a dozen helpers, because he was well fixed. And when a couple of rooms were completed, when the plaster dried, Lizzie joined him in Grayling with two wagons loaded with treasures: her books, her parlor organ, sets of china and silver, chests of linen and silk. She also brought a camera with a black hood to throw over the head to keep out light, stacks of plates, jars of gelatin, bottles of acid and silver chloride. Her Indians had been suspicious of her camera. It had seemed to them that if their ghosts appeared on paper, they had lost something of themselves.

"Don't ever call them all Digger Indians," Lizzie said, "as if they didn't have their own tribes and worth!"

"I won't," John said simply, because he never had.

She had triumphed when the Tehachapi chief consented to sit for her—not so much for her powers of persuasion, but because the Old Indian couldn't imagine Lizzie's hurting anybody. That photograph had appeared in *Leslie's*. The pride and the despair in the old man's eyes were haunting: he knew that the Indians' number was up. Lizzie hoped that the photograph would say what she felt about it.

*

About five years after the ranchers had trailed their herds up from California, Grayling was named seat of a county about the size of Massachusetts. By 1892, fifteen hundred people lived in the town. There was great excitement—the railroad was coming through, maybe within the year. A big crew of men, many of whom were known personally, were making yellow bricks for a courthouse. Ranchers, catching the fever, spoke openly about buying property in town and improving it—expanding, they called it. But John Metlen and Martin Connard had the funds to do it. John built a hotel; Connard built a bank. The railroad came through before either was finished.

The safe in Connard's bank had walls of a new fired brick specified by the Mosler Company. Thieves could scarcely hope to get at it, unless they understood dynamite and had a lot of it. The foot-thick steel door for the safe had arrived on a flatcar; a dozen men with levers and block and tackle raised and shoved and pushed the thing on rollers and moved it inch by inch across South Pacific Street to the Bank. A young fellow hired off the street with good American currency had had his leg crushed in the operation. Connard paid him right off, right on the street with good American currency, and took a release for "value received." The young fellow made no further trouble.

John's hotel was ready to open in May of 1893. It stood but a hundred yards from the Union Pacific depot, handy for drummers to carry over their own grips; but a spring wagon marked HOTEL METLEN in bright red was ready to follow with heavy sample cases or such, or with the steamer trunks that ladies would require.

The hotel had twenty rooms and a bathroom on each of the two upper floors, one for ladies and one for gents. Under one window in each room lay a neat coil of hempen rope—women away from home think a good deal about fires and escaping from them. Should anybody call you on the telephone down at the desk, the clerk could press a button and a bell would tinkle in your room, as soon as the telephone wires were strung down from Butte.

The manager and his wife were already comfortably installed in the hotel. They'd come from Denver, where he had managed a big rooming house. Now the wife attended to the kitchen; the husband ordered supplies, saw to the plumbing and the furnace and walked about pleasantly.

Ten tables in the dining room were covered with white

cloths. A man could get his teeth into the food—roast beef and steaks, halibut brought in from the Coast by train, fried oysters. A woman, sick of fried foods, might choose the chicken salad or poached native rainbow trout. Small wonder the citizens of Grayling were proud of their hotel. They came to sit in the wicker chairs in the lobby, to hear the canary bird in the brass cage. Strangers on the train were bound to sit up and take notice as they pulled into Grayling—even the Pullman passengers who in their lives had seen God knows what.

Ah, but the bar: it was of solid mahogany with a thick brass rail and solid brass cuspidors; the back bar was mahogany, too, with heavy mahogany columns that supported a solid mahogany lintel. The huge mirror was first-class beveled. Over it hung a reproduction of Custer's Last Stand, painted by an old fellow who blew in the first winter. He used a magazine illustration, and was very hard up. Some thought the painting a strange choice, considering Lizzie Metlen and the Indians, but she saw the painting for what it was—an illustration of what happens to a foolish, headstrong man. And anyway, nobody except Lizzie thought much about Indians anymore. In that country, they were done for.

So there it was, the Metlen Hotel, a heavy brick cube, a building to last, whose windows might forever reflect the bloody Western sunset. But what riveted a stranger's eye was the yellow brick tower that rose above the entrance almost a hundred feet—there was nothing taller between Butte and Salt Lake City, not even the grain elevators. Such a tower called for a clock, called for a bell, even a cross, but it was topped by nothing but its flat roof. Was the tower meant for storage space? Not a boy in town but wanted to get up there to see what the world looked like. Yes, you had to hand it to John Metlen for making an impression. No clock, no bell, no cross, but way up there was a sandstone slab, and deeply cut into it was the single word METLEN.

It might have been said of John Metlen that his cup ran over, and that may well have been said. It did not much bother him that he now owed money. He did not speak of this to Lizzie, because women have a tendency to look on money as security. It is not right for a man to disturb a woman.

So his cup ran over.

Very shortly it more than ran over.

They were not young people when the first guest signed the register. Lizzie was thirty-six, John forty-one. For ten years neither had spoken to the other about what was on their minds; she did not speak because that would be to accuse him, and he did not speak because that would be to accuse her (it is not right for a man to disturb a woman), and the fact was they were both awfully lucky to have each other, and to have the sort of understanding the one for the other that prevented their saying what was on their minds. Two such people don't need anything else. They don't need anybody else.

Then one morning very shortly after the first guest had signed the register, they were standing at the window of the sandstone house. The posts of the fences, the corrals, had weathered; grass waved from the sod roof of the barn. A nice collection of broken wheels and wagon parts was gathering in the yard that had been so bare. Lizzie whispered to him. No one was near, but she whispered.

He stepped back and looked directly into her eyes. When he could speak, he said, "Are you sure, Lizzie?"

"Yes. I'm sure."

John Metlen could seldom account for what he thought, let alone what he did. "I'm going to hook up the buggy. Let's drive into town." He wanted to walk the streets and be seen by a great many people.

It was a Sunday morning in June, altogether the most beautiful morning John had ever experienced. Looking up, a man could see three different weathers in the wide sky and choose the one he liked. His fields were green, his Hereford cattle grazing in the mountains; it was ten miles to town and his high-stepping Hambletonians made the trip in less than an hour and no lather to show.

Lizzie had never looked prettier; he had recently been thinking that she looked prettier than usual, and of course she did, because a pregnant lady does look prettier.

They laughed and sang all the way to town.

They handed over the buggy and the team to the young fellow he'd hired to take care of the horses and to meet the trains. And then they began to walk the streets. Not a great many people were on the streets; it was not yet twelve o'clock. Some people were in church, and a good many others were probably still in bed or reading the Butte newspapers that came down on the ten-o'clock train. John would have wished for a street full of men and women who would see them and say later on, "We met the Metlens on the street. Something marvelous must have happened to them."

Just ahead of Lizzie and John walked two young ladies and two young men, couple by couple. Probably twenty feet ahead.

They walked slowly, leisurely, as if the world were theirs; they spoke softly and leaned close. They may have been only a week into courtship, exchanging confidences, each daring at last to offer himself or herself as he truly was or she truly was, and not the attractive enigma of only yesterday, but it's not likely they'd gone much farther than confessing a preference for certain foods and naming a favorite color.

With John and Lizzie following, they approached a door that gave on the sidewalk between the drugstore and the harness shop. Behind it was a flight of stairs, but John had never seen anybody enter or leave there. Traffic to the upper region arrived and departed through a door in the alley behind, approached by steep wooden steps like a fire escape.

The several women who lived up there were not seen on the streets by daylight. They had sandwiches sent over from the Sugar Bowl Café, and late at night, and very early in the morning, and delivered by a young man who washed dishes. Friends questioned him closely.

The windows on the street side, below which the two courting couples and John and Lizzie walked, were heavily curtained with machine-made lace. Anyone with but a fleeting experience with lace curtains knows that lace curtains can be looked out from into the light, but not from the outside in, and those on the inside have the entire advantage. No doubt the young women up there, when not otherwise occupied, looked down into the street and envied the innocence of those who passed below that permitted them to walk under the sun. But no doubt some of those who passed below envied from time to time the depravity of those who lived above, having so often felt that they were missing something.

Certainly something had been going on up there. When the two courting couples had just reached that door, it burst open and a young woman exploded into the street and collided with the four.

A hawk might have plunged among chickens. Surely it was the suddenness of the woman's appearance that caused the young ladies to flatten themselves against the side of the building, touching their lips with their fingers, and not the young woman's lack of morals. But the young men, seeing an opportunity to show their intendeds that they were prepared to shield virtue with their very bodies, moved in such a way that the young woman was knocked into the street. She stumbled, and something fell from her hands.

The young ladies removed their fingers from their lips, surveyed the folds of their dresses, and walked on with the two young men.

The young woman was not dressed at all for the street, nor quite for the bedchamber. John paused. Lizzie approached her.

"Please?" Lizzie said, and knelt, and retrieved a small handbag of cracked patent leather. She handed it to the young woman. "Are you all right, dear?"

The young woman nodded.

"I have a purse very like that," Lizzie said. Her eyes and the young woman's met. Then it was over. John and Lizzie walked on.

"You're lovely," John said.

Lizzie spoke softly and passionately. "She was afraid to pick it up. Afraid of any move to draw attention to herself. Imagine, needing to be invisible. She couldn't speak. It would have been kinder if those two young men had slapped her face. Then at least she wouldn't feel untouchable."

"You're defending her?"

"Understanding, or trying to. And don't pretend you wouldn't come to her rescue. Nobody knows what a person has got to do, what a woman has got to do. I don't know the circumstances, and I thank my stars I never had to make a choice." They walked in silence, and then Lizzie said, "And we're not even certain she's a prostitute."

"What? Not certain? Painted like that? Dressed like that? Then what on earth was she doing up there?"

"Oh, probably visiting."

*

John often looked at his hands; they hadn't seemed to change, but the calendar had. Two years, five years, and then their boy, named Zachary, was six. Six years old, he stood in the dusty road before the big sandstone house with his friend, the same age, the Indian boy. They had been close friends for two years, since they had both realized that a companion makes life even more of an adventure, that pebbles are shinier and minnows easier to capture. They would continue to be friends, but only in the summertime now. In two days Zack Metlen would start school in Grayling, where his father had built another house, and Eagle Foot would be left behind.

That little boy's father, Tendoy, was chief of the Shoshones in that country; as a child himself, Tendoy had attended a mission school run by Jesuits, but that school was long gone, and he would not send his son to a school for whites. White children cared nothing that his son was the son of a chief.

White children saw his son as part of a vanishing race, despised because it could not compete. His son's skin was not like theirs, and his customs were crazy.

Chief Tendoy sensed what is true, that children are innately cruel, and that like cells, they mean to drive out or to destroy the one who is different.

Tendoy had come in his buggy to get his son, who'd been visiting at the Metlen place for two weeks. Chief Tendoy was about thirty-five, lean and wiry; his Asiatic ancestry was evident—he might have been a favored young lieutenant with Genghis Khan, hurrying east on a fast horse to cross the Bering Strait before the ice went out. As chief, he was in touch with the Bureau of Indian Affairs, and probably astonished them back there in Washington by the quality of the letters he sent them, all carefully edited by Lizzie.

That first week of September the frost lay heavy each morning over the stubble in the fields, and smoke from distant forest fires hung about the mountain peaks, and drifted down. It was a sad time for the two small friends. When they wandered up from the creek where they'd been playing, Tendoy spoke in Shoshone to his son, and in English to Zack.

"You boys have a foot race?"

Both recognized it not as a question but as an order.

John, who stood with Tendoy on the porch, thought a foot race a poor conclusion to the summer, a summer that marked the beginning of a long parting, a summer remembered as a time when one boy won, and one boy lost, one conquered, one was vanquished, a summer that might leave them not friends but competitors.

The two little boys went out into the dusty road and stood side by side.

"Race to the fence," Tendoy ordered. "Go!"

Zack was badly beaten and, curiously, seemed not to mind. Afterward they all sat in the deep green shade of the hopvines that crawled up each year on the heavy hempen string against the porch of the big house. Tendoy sipped his iced tea and set down his glass. He had made no comment on the outcome of the foot race. Now he said, "A dream came to me once." Before his boy was born, he said, he saw a child with wings on his feet, and that is what happened. The wings could not be seen—as the camera might see them—because if the wings could be seen, other fathers would be envious.

Eagle Foot stood by his father, watching, waiting for orders.

Except that Tendoy spoke among friends and in the shade of hopvines that enclosed a private world where anything might be said, John would have felt embarrassed for Tendoy, that he should speak with the innocence of a child, and so be vulnerable to an adult's scorn. Wasn't it the Indians' reliance on dreams and not on reality that had ruined them? However, whatever John's dreams were for Zack, after the foot race one of Tendoy's dreams had already been vindicated. It hardly mattered that the world had now so changed for the Indians that fleetness of foot counted for nothing.

"But all is good," Tendoy murmured, smiling, triumphant. "I think your boy be rich."

Both John and Lizzie glanced at Zack. That Zack would be rich was more than possible. In the eyes of many, he already was rich—ten thousand fertile acres, a stout roof over his head, a room set aside for books . . .

"And I think," Tendoy continued, "he marry."

That, too, was more than possible. Certainly possible considering Zack's background. Why had Tendoy, usually rather closemouthed, spoken of marriage as somehow unusual? Under the spell of the deep green shade, Lizzie wondered if Tendoy did indeed have a special knowledge of the future, and, like those who wish to believe, she put reason aside for a moment, and believed that because the Indians were so privy to Nature, so familiar with the lightning stalking the plain for victims, so in communication with the murmur of underground waters (you heard them down at the far end of the caves where the Indians buried the dead), that Nature whispered secrets to Indians unguessed by whites.

"What do you mean," she asked, "that he will marry?"

Thinking, What a foolish woman I am, to so love my child that I will listen even to dreams and nonsense.

John, too, had been considering the arcane, but he was so aware of his own irrational concern with signs and portents he felt he must make light of them. "Lizzie," he said, and he spoke most reasonably, "Tendoy means that Zack will marry and have children to help him and to honor him and to win races. That way they might even have wings on their feet." He smiled, and then he laughed, but his own laugh sounded strange to him. "Isn't that what you mean, Tendoy? Isn't that it?"

Suddenly from the upper reaches of Black Canyon a wind blew down and seized the hopvines and shook them.

In a moment Tendoy said, "No. Not that."

Chapter
2

Shortly after the Metlens had established themselves in their new house in Grayling so that Zack could attend school, John took the train to Denver for the livestock show. He wanted to look around for a few Hereford bulls of the Domino strain. He liked Denver; it was the biggest city between St. Louis and the Coast, and the jewelry stores there had a good selection of emeralds. He meant to buy another one for Lizzie, this time in celebration of Zack's starting school—another milestone. Anyway, he loved to give, loved the light in people's eyes.

He put up again at the Brown Palace; he liked good hotels. He was new at the hotel business, and although his hotel, Lord knows, was on a far smaller scale than the Brown Palace, he felt that it offered a man the opportunity to get up slowly, have a shave and get into a good suit of clothes with a fresh collar, come downstairs, shoulders back, eat a good hearty breakfast, pay for it, leave a generous tip and then saunter into the lobby. There he'd sit with a panatela—García y Vega or Antonio y Cleopatra—comfortable and at ease, watching the world go by. That morning at the Brown Palace, before he went downstairs, there had come a little tap on his door. When he opened it, he found, perfect, pristine and flat, the *Rocky Mountain News*. He thought, What a capital idea, and filed it away for his own hotel.

By the time the stores had opened, he was on the street in his good suit of clothes and fresh white collar, shoulders back, having eaten a good hearty breakfast. On that street he stood suddenly amazed.

In a window was the most magnificent toy in the world. Two armies, Union and Confederate, of more than fifty men each, faced each other on a field of real, honest earth. Each side had a general, two captains, and sergeants galore. Some foot soldiers stood, some knelt, aiming rifles. Cavalry swept in from the rear on both sides; teams of Percherons and Clydesdales brought up cannon. It appeared the cannon might shoot birdshot—and well, they did. The cannon had iny springs inside, and triggers to release them. He found out because he went inside.

The young clerk was extremely frank and honest and would probably go far.

"We don't really expect anybody to buy it," he said. "But .here have been inquiries."

That was because of the cost.

"I wonder if you'd let me see a few pieces?"

"I'd be glad to." The decent young man leaned into the space behind the window and brought out two pieces, a cannon among them. "Wouldn't it be fine to be young again."

"If you don't expect anybody to buy it, why is it in the window?"

The young man laughed. "Because it brings people inside."

"Yes, of course. You're a bunch of rascals. I wonder what price you have on it."

The young man told him.

John whistled.

"You see, every face is hand-painted," the young man explained. And each soldier—because a hand and not a machine had created him—had the fault of personality.

"The tails on the horses," John said.

"That's real hair, sir."

"Those flags."

"Silk, sir. This is the box—wait till I find it."

Polished hardwood, the sides dovetailed, the hinges of brass and screwed on, not nailed. When the armies were locked inside, the box could be hidden. Whoever looked at the box knew, because of the lock, that what was inside was valuable.

"Thank you," John said. "I hope I wasn't a trouble."

"You certainly weren't, sir. I guess you have a boy."

"Yes. I have a boy."

"I have a girl. I guess a girl wouldn't care for it. I've got no excuse, even if I had the money."

John began to walk back to the Brown Palace Hotel. How foolish it would have been to buy such a thing. The first thing that would happen, a piece would get lost. And you would know, even if you tried to forget, that the army was no longer complete. It had been spoiled. So you'd have to remove one of the pieces from the other side, and make it even. But not complete. Ruined.

It was not the money. He could afford it. It was just that it was simply out of proportion. The two perfect armies were not meant to be bought. The young man had said as much.

"We don't expect anybody to buy it."

Clever of them.

No child would have expected his father to buy such a thing. A child would as soon expect his father to buy him an elephant. Some things are possible, and some are not.

And anyway, buying the thing for a child would set a terrible example; the child would then come to expect too much of the future. And it would be the father's fault, wouldn't it?

Though any father who passed that shop alone might have gone in, to make inquiry. For there had been inquiries. The young clerk wouldn't have said there had been inquiries if there hadn't been. He did not strike John as that sort of fellow.

How glad John was to be approaching his room in the Brown Palace Hotel. But first he would sit in the lobby and watch the world go by. One or two who passed would surely stop to gaze at that toy in the window.

Unless, of course, it was no longer there.

Why, even at this moment, some other father might be preparing to make good his "inquiry," wanting his child to have a gift no other child possessed. Right at this very moment, that man might be putting his hand upon his checkbook.

John stopped in his tracks, and turned.

*

The house in town was just a house. At Christmas, they went home to the ranch.

As usual, John had picked out just the right Christmas tree in the early fall when he trailed cattle down from the range to winter pasture and there wasn't yet a flake of snow in the Big Hole Valley. No one knew he picked out his trees so early; they'd have thought him foolish. Early in the morning of the day before Christmas he hitched up the team to a sleigh, threw in an ax and a jar of hot coffee, and away he went. And Lizzie said, as she said every year, "It doesn't take you long to find a good tree, John. Does it?"

"Well, you have to find one in the open, where the sun gets around."

Lizzie had the mincemeat made up from lean venison,

raisins, apples, citron and honey and a dollop of good brandy. Mince pies were a part of her tradition. John remembered two eggnogs, one made with whiskey for the men and one with sherry for the women. But that was back in California. Here in Montana, people in town saw people in town, and nobody dropped in way out here at the ranch on Christmas Eve. Lizzie and John would have a brandy punch and maybe, later, a piece of her pie before they went to bed: cold milk's the thing with pie. They would go softly past the door where their child slept. Were they not lucky?

Every Christmas morning the cook rang the triangle out back and the hired men trooped in. It was still dark outside, stars bright, dogs barking near the barn, when they sat down at the long table in the back dining room and found again this year the square envelope at each and every plate.

The cards had been Lizzie's idea. "A check alone's so cold, John."

And the men liked the cards because they could open them and then be surprised.

"Hey now. Look here!"

Surprised is easier than grateful, and less embarrassing to all.

If they could get to town that night, if there wasn't a storm brewing in Black Canyon, by the next morning the checks would be lying flat in the till of a saloon in Grayling or folded and tucked in a whore's stocking. John didn't judge. He didn't need booze, didn't need to forget, didn't need to feel for a little while—as long as the booze lasted—like a man to be reckoned with. It was damned mean how the unfortunate make a man feel fortunate. He was married to the best woman in the world and he had a son. Maybe somewhere they did, too. You didn't ask.

John was glad to escape after breakfast to the front dining room; mahogany and silver, a fire in the fireplace in the room beyond, and Lizzie having coffee.

*

By seven o'clock the polished pendulum of the tall clock in the living room reflected like a figure eight the pale light of dawn. Zack was still asleep. Only six years old, he wasn't yet expected to be up for breakfast with the men.

"It must have been very expensive," Lizzie said.

Did he detect criticism? Concern? She hadn't seen the armies before; he'd had the box sent directly from the shop. They'd promised it would arrive on time, that it would be properly insured; but leaving Denver, he had at once regretted having it shipped. If it was lost, insurance would be cold comfort. It was irreplaceable. Money isn't much use unless it will replace—exactly. But how could he have taken it with him? Questions! Questions from Zack: a child is curious about packages. Selfish little beasts, children assume, since they are loved, that what's in a box is theirs. Questions from Lizzie. Yes, from the first he felt she would disapprove. He wasn't sure why, but there was even a gritty residue of doubt in his own mind when he left the shop for the first time and walked back toward the hotel.

"No," he told her now, "it wasn't cheap." He had often erred in assuming that honesty excuses poor judgment.

"These pieces are hand-carved, John." When she addressed him as John, he got wary.

He examined a piece. "They do look so."

"Each piece has a personality."

"Yes, they do seem to have."

"John, I'd say this outfit represents a good part of some man's life."

An ugly thought intruded. Lizzie was right. No man could have afforded to create such pieces—even for the price John had paid—only a man who had no future but the completion of this outrageous toy. He knew such work. It came from behind the gray stone walls of the state penitentiary—a watch chain so intricately braided of black horsehair it resembled flexible jet; snakelike ropes and whips of rawhide; silver work as fragile as frost on leaves—all of it the end of desperate dedication, a hiding place from the horror of the past, present and future. He hoped no such thought had prompted Lizzie's remark that the soldiers were a good part of a stranger's life. She did not say what he knew she was thinking—should a child have a toy that has sapped a man's life?

She said only, "Let me wrap it."

So it was wrapped the morning before Christmas, and the next morning it was unwrapped—and to no joy that John could see. Zack examined the cannon. He removed the tiny springs; he replaced them. Then he set the whole thing aside.

That night when Zack had gone upstairs to bed, John brought Lizzie a glass of sherry and poured himself a whiskey. "Damn it, Lizzie, I don't know my own son."

"Oh now, John."

"Well, maybe I bought the thing for myself."

"Maybe a little of that," she said. "But not much. You don't think much about yourself."

How wrong she was.

She continued, "It's too old for a child. He doesn't appreciate what's special, each face different, each soldier an individual. That whoever carved it . . ." She paused.

He finished for her. "That whoever carved it was something like God."

What Zack appreciated and had carried up to bed with him was a trifle sent along in the box from Lizzie's father— a small horseshoe magnet with a bright red handle, and a little iron rod.

Chapter
3

That Lizzie Metlen carried the torch for the Indians was well known, and in their hearts people accorded her the respect people feel for those who support the plundered, the failed and the defeated. But surely even Lizzie Metlen realized by now that the Indians in this country were doomed—doomed as in fact they had been doomed the moment the first Pilgrim set foot on Plymouth Rock. The whites wanted what the Indians had, and with guns and tricks, they got it. Now there was no place in American society for Indians, except as interesting freaks in circuses and road shows. Yes, people did admire Lizzie, but it is not at all pleasant to admire somebody who is on the losing side—he himself appears to lose.

One morning late in June with school out for the summer, Lizzie, with a trowel in her hand, knelt near the headgate to one side of the big house; the headgate would raise water in the irrigation ditch so that it flowed into a smaller ditch and reached the cottonwoods she'd planted, and a blue spruce sent out from Wisconsin. The cottonwoods she'd planted as saplings, and now they cast real shadows. Their leaves whispered.

Rain had fallen the night before, and the damp soil exuded seminal odors and the air was rich with the promise of growth. Lizzie was transplanting bluebells she'd brought down from a nearby hill. In the past she'd had little luck—none. Like peonies, the bluebells disliked being moved; they wilted, lingered long enough to inspire hope and then they died in the new surroundings. But Lizzie disliked having failed, and this year she hoped to trick them into believing they had not been moved, by so digging them up that their roots were entirely enclosed in their own familiar earth.

She paused and turned.

John rode up before the house on a bay horse; he'd spent the night in Grayling at his hotel, supervising or something. He seldom rode up to the front of the house. His habit was to put away his horse in the barn.

What was up? Lizzie smiled. "You're a pleasant surprise."

John swung down off the bay horse and draped the bridle reins over the top pole of the low fence meant to keep wandering livestock from Lizzie's California poppies. Then he walked in through the gate and sat down on the steps of the porch like a tired man. She sat beside him.

"What's wrong?"

He removed his hat, and he raked his fingers through his hair. "I hear the government's moving the Indians off to a reservation."

She said, "Then it appears that somebody thinks it's easier to drive the Indians off their land than to come to honorable terms with them."

"I guess that's it."

"But even the government isn't so heartless as to drive them off without a reason. Unless there is some 'incident' they've seized on."

John looked at the hat in his hand, and then across the valley. "There was an incident."

"You mean recently?"

"No."

"The old incident, then. Last summer."

A haystack had been set ablaze in the middle of a field, in the middle of the night, and it was sobering to watch it burn like an enormous torch there where nothing before had ever been seen to burn.

A young Indian had been arrested. He had been arrested because he could not account for his whereabouts when the flames shot up, and as an Indian he had reason to resent and to damage the property of a white man. Of course, the criminal might have been a tramp who had been turned away, or a hired man who had been fired.

But the young Indian had been heard to make threats of some kind against the whites, in a barroom, where he had no right to be. It was illegal to sell an Indian a drink, and it was illegal for an Indian to drink it. It was presumed that, unlike the whites, Indians, when they drank, became inflamed.

The tramp who had been turned away, or the disgruntled hired man, had long gone into some other situation, but the young Indian was now at the federal prison in Leavenworth, in Kansas, maybe forever. Chief Tendoy had not been able to save him. Kansas is a long way off; Kansas is without trees and mountains.

John said, "You don't seem much upset."

"I'm not. Because I intend to draw up a petition, and have our friends sign it. Washington listens to petitions, when they're from the right quarter. We are not without power."

"I am sorry to say," John said, "I have bad news. It's too late for petitions. The President has already signed papers."

"I don't believe it. It takes months, years, for such papers to reach the President—red tape. Hearings and the Bureau of Indian Affairs *after* the Department of the Interior. It would have been in the papers. We'd have heard."

"I'm saying just what I heard."

"Did you hear who said the President had signed papers?"

"They say Martin Connard."

"I see. And it was his haystack. And, John, he's lying."

"I shouldn't care to tell him that."

"I don't mind. Liars don't deserve deference. He's afraid of a petition. He doesn't want one started. He wants the world to believe the departure of the Indians is as good as accomplished."

"Isn't it?"

"Of course not. I'm going to Connard in the morning and call his bluff."

John hesitated. "Want me to go along?"

"No. I'm my own woman. I suppose it's that the Indians are more my concern. And it's natural for a woman to show compassion. She isn't embarrassed by compassion." She smiled at him.

*

She swept into the north of town next morning in her stylish Studebaker buggy, stylish herself in a gray suit and gray hat and a veil. She drove well, and the black Hambletonians stepped high and it was exactly the kind of day to go forth and see justice was done.

She first passed, in the north of town, their own house, built in 1902 when Zack became of school age; it was white and frame and substantial, but nothing at all to compare with Martin Connard's house far on down the street, which was the showpiece of the town. Only in Butte, sixty miles to the north, where the Copper Kings built chateaux and palazzi, did a sheltering structure approach it in size and elegance. It was of the same red brick as Connard's bank, where she would beard the man in his office. The iron stag standing on the lawn of Connard's house might be taken for real. It stood with raised head, nose testing the weather. Curious children were thwarted by a high iron fence finished off with sharp spikes.

Connard's own child, a boy of ten and a year older than

Zack, was just as dark as Zack was towheaded. This child did not attend Grayling Public School but lived with his aunt during the school year in a house with pillars on Queen Anne Hill in Seattle, and the aunt returned him each year by Pullman car to Grayling, and standing tall she watched their luggage removed from the baggage car, her lips counting— she was her brother's sister. The boy, Harry, was hardly seen in town; a buggy drawn by sorrell Orloff trotters flew into town for him. On the Connard ranch, it was said, he "be-haved like a wild Indian."

"Poor little tyke," a lady was heard to murmur over the whist table. "Poor little motherless tyke." Just so, she established herself as trustworthy among the ladies, and in line for Connard goodwill. The tyke's mother had died in childbirth, and much is excused a child who has so lost his dam.

The tyke was tall for his age, and the men out there on the Connard ranch were afraid of him—afraid that should an accident involve a horse or some high place, they'd be held responsible. It was a Connard principle that somebody is ultimately responsible and of course, everybody is. It was said that young Harry Connard respected only the ranch foreman, and that old Connard had given the foreman the right to thrash the boy, if necessary, for his own good. Who is not the better for an early acquaintance with the sharp sting of discipline? But so far as anybody knew, no thrashing had ever come about. Of course, the boy was different—Queen Anne Hill, the aunt, and that private school said to accept only the sons of millionaires. It was not doubted for a moment in Grayling that such a school existed, because it was never doubted that millionaires exist. If millionaires were content to send their sons to your regular schools, to suffer the inept disciplines of your Miss Merchants and the sarcasms of your Mr. Ogrens, what was the point of being the son of a millionaire? Millionaires need an education that prepares them to wield their awesome power as effectively and humanely as possible.

John Metlen and Martin Connard, the one with his hotel,

and the other with his bank, were the first to bring big money into the town; others followed, and built two- or even three-story brick structures called "blocks" and capped them with cornices hewn from local sandstone and inscribed deep with their names and a date—not in your trendy Arabic numerals but in timeless Roman.

RIFE
MCMI

Rife and Bart and Shineberger (a long name to etch in stone) let space in their blocks for offices, businesses, and showrooms. Now the town of Grayling might choose between two drugstores, and between two young doctors, both admired because everybody knows how hard it is to become a doctor, the corpses and so on, and the study of Latin, and the burden of secrets cast upon them by the sick and the dying.

The town had so grown and so many Scandinavians had taken up small farms in the country around that many more died than used to, and an undertaker had found it worth his while and he came with his knives and pumps and his adjustable cooling table. He set out barrels, like everybody else, for the garbage man. He was most active in the wintertime, when human resistance falters from lack of sun and hope is at low ebb. His name was Brundiger; he looked very like Theodore Roosevelt, recently President, and he wore similar rimless spectacles that flashed. He flashed perfect teeth, and there was no escaping him.

Grayling was now a town to go to, to see, to be seen. Into town came cooks from the ranches, and hired girls; they ate steaks and stews at the Sugar Bowl Café, with Booths for Ladies with green baize curtains to pull across so that your feet alone could be seen. Drummers in fancy duds blew into town and stopped at the Metlen Hotel and moved through the countryside in buggies hired from the livery stable; they showed their nuts and bolts and mechanical devices that might add years to your life. Lightning rods were popular

among those who expected the worst to happen simply because that's what did; it was not foolish to believe one might
be singled out and struck dead, and drummers carried in
folders photographs of dwellings reduced to ash, of splintered property, all for the want of lengths of braided copper
wire and a few spear-shaped rods.

Sheepherders from the Mormon outfits south of town appeared on Saturday nights to get drunk; their dogs sat watching. The sheepherders were Basques and Rumanians.
Mexican section hands shot pool in the Pheasant Lounge, and
like the Rumanians and the Basques they slipped away when
loudmouthed cowboys shouldered in and threatened trouble
for folks who didn't talk United States. In rooms up over the
City Drug, whores got ready with their curling irons and
tweezers. They were, all of them, whores and sheepherders
and cowboys and tellers in the bank, transients; they fed on
each other, but in the end they all fed the original families and
the sons-in-law and the daughters-in-law. Those alone were
not transient and knew that Christmas would be in the same
place and who would bury them and who would get what part
of what remained behind. Aristocracy is a local matter, as valid
in Butte or Grayling as in New York or Boston; its core is who
got there first and profited. Nobody in Boston had heard of a
Connard or a Metlen, and nobody in Grayling had heard
much of Carver or a Saltonstall. But both Metlens and Carvers
knew what the land looked like before houses, and both Saltonstalls and Connards knew the Indians.

She who stood looking into the window of Huber's Jewelry
was no aristocrat; that she was bewitched was evident in her
face above the rows of watches and cheap rings. She stood
alone, but somewhere in the town and not far away, Lizzie
was sure, was the man with whom she'd come in from the
country. For she was pitifully young and not the kind to
brave the town alone.

Her shoes were worn, but clean; her rusty dress was im-
maculate but nondescript, and the jabot at her throat was
tired. But her taffy-colored hair was queenly, a thick braid

coiled about her head in a high gleaming crown as ethnic, as Norwegian, as her high cheekbones. But alas, atop that masterpiece of hair the young woman had placed a hat, because that's what you did when you went to town. The hat sat precarious, a little brimmed pot of black varnished straw, and the red bow, that set it apart from many other hats, trembled. But this child understood propriety absolutely. Of her no one could ever remark, "She stood alone on the street and wore no hat!"

Lizzie's team walked now, the black Hambletonians nodding their heads like circus horses. As Lizzie passed, the young woman turned from the window, as if summoned, and her eyes and Lizzie's eyes met, and held a second or two. Both smiled, as strangers will, each recognizing the other as another human being and worthy of sight, and that moment was suddenly set apart. Lizzie drove on, and as she drove there sat in her mind a conviction that she had misinterpreted the young woman's glance, and she was convinced that something or other was incomplete. It seemed almost as if she should go back and speak. She did not; she drove on to Connard's bank.

CONNARD
MCMXCV

The two tellers inside were caged behind stout brass bars; they were two aging young men who wore low on their foreheads green celluloid eyeshades that cast a pallor over their nether features and, like blinders on a horse, cut from their view all but the business at hand—the close scrutiny of signatures and the counting out of currency. On their right index fingers they wore soft rubber thimbles so that they had no need to spit there. It was sobering to consider how much money passed across their palms, and not much comfort to consider how little of it passed to them who handled it. It might be that they had handled so much of it they had now a contempt for it, but not such

contempt that one does not hear of just such men decamp-
ing to South America with splendid sums. Maybe it was
enough for those two in Connard's bank to know, along
with Connard himself, just exactly how much money you
had, whether you were to be treated casually, or with deference; and yet, as you stood before them—perhaps doubt-
ing yourself—they seemed no more impressed with a
deposit of ten thousand dollars than of one or two dollars.
Such, perhaps, was a result of their training. They were
two aging young men set apart in Grayling, and they and
the wives they could hardly afford visited only each other's
houses.

The main floor of the bank was of black slate flagstones
set in concrete. Heels of leather and those tapped with steel
plates to prevent uneven wear announced your echoing
presence. But in the anteroom outside Connard's office, all
was carpeted; you who had just been so loud might now be
a cat on velvet. Connard was shielded from the impertinent
by a Mrs. Blinn, whose footloose husband had been lost in
the Spanish War. The government had telegraphed her no
dismal announcement of his death, and when she wrote to
those same people long after everybody else was back
home from Cuba, they named him only "missing."

"What a shame for her, not to know."

Not knowing, she could not feel the bleak comfort of widow's weeds. Not knowing, she found remarriage was out of the
question. Not knowing, she could not dispose of his clothes.
But she took the bit in her teeth and at the new university she
learned to be a typewriter. She had always been neat and clean.

"Mr. Connard has been terribly tied up all day," she told
Lizzie. "But I'm as good as certain he'll see you just as soon as
he isn't."

Lizzie believed he'd see her whenever he'd got an argument
together. He certainly must know her reason for seeing him.

"I certainly do admire your understanding that machine,"
she said. "It must be terribly hard to find the right . . ."

"Key," Mrs. Blinn said. "They're called keys, just like a

piano. Yes, it was hard at first, but they blindfolded us. That was our examination."

"When you were blindfolded, did you put the paper in?"

"Oh yes. It's called the Touch System. You do it that way."

"It's wonderful to see women like yourself taking the place of men in business."

Mrs. Blinn flushed. "I'm sure it will be some time before you see a man typewriter. Men are so clumsy. Their fingers, you know. I think I hear Mr. Connard now."

A door opened.

"Come in, won't you, Mrs. Metlen."

And had she been a man, she'd have been intimidated. For the men who came to see Barrett wanted only one thing—money in some guise or another. And anybody who wants or who needs money is at a disadvantage and must be prepared to be refused, prepared to argue and to beg, and prepared to be shown the door. The man who needs money comes with hat in hand, respectful and afraid. A man who needs money is inferior to a man who has it to give, and this is understood all over the world.

The man who needs money should not need it. Had he acted correctly in the past, had he been wise, had he saved, had he considered the future and learned from the past, he would not need it. He would, in fact, have it to give, and he would be sitting on the other side of the desk. But he has lived beyond his means. At the very best, he stands there asking for money to fund some crazy scheme, or to pull somebody's chestnuts out of the fire.

But Lizzie Metlen was not intimidated; she was armed with morals, and had never in her life needed money.

"I will, Mr. Connard. I will come in." She rose and smiled, and she extended her hand. She was proud of her rings; she counted on them. Of her hands without them, she was not so proud. She didn't like gloves when she gardened; she liked the feel of the soil; the tips of her fingers were keen to warmth and moisture; her hands were tanned and they were dry. But it doesn't matter what your hands look like if your rings are good. Dear John.

Connard stood aside and bowed her into his office. She had wondered what it would look like, and now that she saw it, she was again glad of her rings. She wondered if any woman had ever before entered there—his wife, perhaps, when she was alive, but even she would have had but little business there. It was a big room, crowded with furniture and shadows, meant to impress. Every heavy piece appeared to be of black walnut or rosewood; the plush draperies tied back with tasseled cords announced that red is a man's color.

"Please sit down, Mrs. Metlen."

"Thank you." She sat opposite a dark desk. He sat, made a tent of his fingers, a precise enclosing structure. She smiled. His hands suggested play in the nursery.

> This is the church, and this is the steeple
> Open the doors, and there's all the people.

But Connard was no child. He gazed across his fingers as over a gunsight. "To what do I owe this?" he asked.

Behind him was a rack of guns, rifles and shotguns that suggested to visitors that although it had been some time now, he had crouched in the willows holding a shotgun, waiting for the first sun to break across the lake.

To one side, through glass doors in a bookcase, she noted the Tenth Edition of the *Britannica;* she had heard that Connard, like John, had largely educated himself. The volumes here were proof that Connard had all knowledge within reach. A globe a foot in diameter, tilted at that angle so difficult to explain, rested on ball-and-claws, testifying to Connard's global concerns. How many who had entered that room had broken open a *Britannica* or could explain the tilt of the earth?

"I've come about our Indians."

"Mrs. Metlen, the Indians' day is done."

"In some parts of this country, possibly. I've come in fairness to the Indians that you and I both know as friends. Mr. Connard, you and I came into this land, and it was already occupied."

"Occupation implies a proper use, Mrs. Metlen."

"Ah, yes. And hasn't use got to be defined? If a land is used for a life, for happiness—isn't that a proper use? Mr. Connard, had we come into another part of this country, not this part, we might all of us have been murdered in our beds years ago, as trespassers. That was not true, here. But we remain trespassers. Parvenus."

"Parvenus?"

His inflexion told her not that he was questioning whether or not they were parvenus, but rather that he was unfamiliar with the word. The word had slipped out; she had not meant to humiliate him, to question his intelligence. The volumes here at his right hand would tell him, say, which of all the Latin dialects—Rumanian, Portuguese, Spanish, Italian, French—differed most from the mother tongue. From those books he could learn what French was, but not learn it. When the cards were down, the real class distinction was that between the formally educated and the others.

"Upstarts, Mr. Connard. We're Johnnies-come-lately."

"They burned my hay, Mrs. Metlen."

"They? One young Indian. You had it stacked. You didn't plant it. You cast no seed. In this country the hay is wild, given to one and all."

"You're something of a poetess, Mrs. Metlen."

"Suppose that we were about to be dispossessed by the Indians? Suppose the shoe was on the other foot?"

"The shoe is not on the other foot. The shoe is on our foot."

"On yours, possibly. Oh, we whites have the power, but power is ugly when turned on the powerless. But suppose we no longer spar? I intend to start a petition. I assure you it will be signed by men and women in this valley whom you respect and trust. I intend to travel about. The names of our friends will announce their fairness—and shall we say gratitude?

Thankful that they were not murdered in their beds, but were allowed to live in peace.

"But I have heard, Mr. Connard, that the matter is settled, that the Indians are about to be sent away to Fort Hall. I have heard that the President has signed certain papers, and that it is you who have said that the President has done this."

"That is correct."

"The President has signed papers?"

"That is my understanding."

"Understanding is not certainty. You are certain?"

"Yes, Mrs. Metlen."

"Then you will not object if I call the President by telephone."

"I don't object. But I doubt that the President —"

"You doubt that the President of the United States would attend the small, unfamiliar voice of Elizabeth Metlen in Grayling, Montana. That anyone, especially a woman, could expect the President to pick up the telephone to hear her. But we shall see, we shall see. I don't think in the scheme of things that my husband and I are powerless in this land." She glanced down at her rings. "And when I speak to the President, then I shall have the knowledge, and not the understanding. I shall see then how the earth tilts." She rose and smiled, and extended her hand. "Good afternoon, Mr. Connard."

When she rose, he rose; it had been long since anyone had seen behind his beard, but his eyes told all. He spoke. "One moment, Mrs. Metlen. I must ask you. Does your husband know you're here?"

"Yes," she said. "Certainly he knows."

His question was not a question. It was a threat, and Connard was too cautious a man to make a threat where there was nothing to be threatened.

But. But he would not have made a threat even if there was something to be threatened if he were not lying about the President's knowing. She was certain he had been lying when it turned out to be almost three years later that the

Indians left; had he not been lying, had the papers already been signed, the Indians would have been expelled within weeks. Oh, later she realized she had held more cards than Connard had, and better cards.

For of all things, a banker must be known as honest; money insists that it be in charge of an honest man. And one telegram to Washington was bound to expose Connard as a liar. Then her petition would have gone forward and the Indians would have been saved.

Connard might then have argued that it was best and most profitable for his depositors that the Indians be deprived of their lands and homes and rights, but he would be seen as a liar. If a man lies about one thing, he will lie about another.

Deposits would be withdrawn.

Yes. Not far away there were other banks. Honest banks.

But she had made no further move. She had not even picked up the telephone.

"Yes," she had said. "Certainly he knows, Mr. Connard." But in that moment she recalled in pristine clarity John's hesitation in riding out to see Connard.

John was afraid of something. Past or future.

And what that thing was became clear when Connard spoke. "Does your husband know you're here?"

Was it the hotel? John did spend a good deal of time in the office of the hotel at the rolltop desk. She disliked the idea of money and left a room to avoid hearing the rip of checks torn out.

Their sandstone house—so grand she felt ridiculous descending the circular staircase on some foolish errand like poking up the fire. "Palatial," the *Grayling Examiner* had described the house on the front page, an article about the party they'd given when they moved into their "palatial" house.

Looking now at her rings, she saw them in quite a different light, in such a light as Connard must have seen them when she held her hand to him.

So—she did nothing. She thought only to protect John

and her boy. In doing so, she had probably thrown the Indians to the wolves.

Yes. She could possibly with one telephone call have ruined Connard. But he could ruin John.

*

First the government men rounded up the Indians and herded them like sheep into a camp under the foothills ten miles west of the Metlen ranch. Then they took a census; absent members of the tribe were hunted down in the hills by United States marshals. The government provided food, sacks of potatoes, sacks of beans, slabs of bacon, salt. The days of fresh meat were over.

The government also provided new canvas tents and helped the Indians put them up; they were more complicated than Indian wickiups. They were aligned in streets and avenues; all was neat and clean and military. There weren't any dogs. The dogs must be left behind. To their credit, the marshals were circumspect, but they made their presence and their rifles known. The last campfires in that country burned low. The willows along the creeks had long since turned a rusty red; the ground squirrels were holing up. Only occasionally would you see one sitting on its own mound of earth straight as a picket pin against the horizon. Each morning the creeks wore a thin skin of ice that sagged and melted by noon; but not so early next morning. A first snow had fallen in the mountain passes.

Several times Lizzie and John had driven out to this camp, guests of Tendoy's. Guests, indeed. She could hardly speak civily to the marshals. She and John had made plans to go again before the posted date of the Indians' departure. They meant to bring gifts.

Then, suddenly, they were visited by Tendoy and his boy. At least, she and Zack were. John was away in a new Lozier motorcar he'd bought.

Tendoy and his boy rode up bareback on sorrel ponies that wore hackamores instead of bridles. The whites never understood hackamores, which controlled a horse with the pressure of a complicated knot that pressed up against the lower jaw; the whites used bits in bridles that cut a tender mouth and gouged the tongue.

Tendoy wore his big black hat, crown uncreased, black woolen trousers that John had given him at Christmas, and elaborately beaded moccasins. The boy was called Joe now instead of Eagle Foot by the Norwegians in the country school. He alone among the Indians attended that school. What did the Norwegians know of dreams and totems? The boy wore bib overalls and a red flannel shirt; his twisted tweed cap was pulled low. He sat straight.

"Get down, get down, my friends! Get down and come inside."

They tied their horses to the fence out front.

She called to Zack up the circular staircase; he and she and John had come out to the ranch for the weekend. Zack was in his room among his batteries and wires. "Come down. Tendoy and Eagle Foot!"

Tendoy scorned chairs; he and the boy hunkered down, he on the right side of the fireplace and the boy on the left. The hired girl brought in coffee and cups from the kitchen. Tendoy removed his black hat and set it beside him. The boy removed his cap, watching his father. Tendoy nodded. Tendoy seemed never to have heard of the drug caffeine; he allowed the boy coffee.

Lizzie said, "Will you have coffee, Zack?"

He looked astonished. "Yes, thank you." This had never happened to him before. He glanced at Eagle Foot. Eagle Foot so held his cup that it warmed his hands.

"We come to say goodbye," Tendoy said, looking at nobody.

"To say goodbye!"

"We go early morning."

"But I thought—Tendoy, I thought . . ."

"Marshals afraid of trouble in camp. Rifle missing. They count. Some crazy fool," Tendoy said.

"To say goodbye!" She had thought that maybe Tendoy believed she and John had visited the camp out of compunction for what she had done or, rather, what she had not done. But now it was cruelly clear that Tendoy had no idea of what she had done—not done. That proud spirit and that proud little boy would never have passed through her doorway had they any idea she had betrayed them. Oh, but she hated herself. Her voice was a false voice. She hated it. "I'm sick that John isn't here. He drove to Butte in his new machine." What must Tendoy make of such an expensive contraption?

"You tell him goodbye from me." Tendoy removed himself from the world in the complicated business of rolling a cigarette.

The boy had hardly taken his eyes from his father. Lizzie saw he found support there in what had become alien surroundings—this living room where once he had been at home.

And Zack stared at his shoes. Did Zack know anything of her deceit? Anything? Nothing. Of course he knew nothing!

"Then, is Eagle Foot a prince?" That's what Zack had asked when he was nine, like the child of a primitive people who could not imagine government without kings—fathers of their people—people who required the assurance of dynasty as some require the assurance of God, someone to turn to.

For she had remarked that Tendoy, as chief of the Shoshones, was like a king. She had meant to make clear that Zack was never to look on Eagle Foot as other than superior. Eagle Foot had blood. At nine, Zack had relished the idea of kings. A child of nine can hardly respect presidents and prime ministers who can vanish before you blink an eye. But kings survive, and kings wear crowns they pass on. Zack had made a crown of an old felt hat.

"Yes," she told him. "You could truly say that Eagle Foot is a prince."

But the two boys had grown apart since Zack had moved

into Grayling for school. Loyal as Zack was, they would surely have drifted apart anyway when it was clear that the Indians, because of poverty and lack of "ambition," were no longer comfortable companions. Just so, white children in the South drifted away from once-loved colored folk and assigned them their "proper" role of servant and dependent. Friends of youth disappeared. And it was not always they whom you missed, but yourself as you were.

Such must account for Zack's present gloom. Except to speak of the coffee, he'd said not a word. The two boys might have been strangers, each one embarrassed by Time Passed: one of them the real prince with a father off touring in a Lozier motor car, with twenty thousand acres and a brick hotel, the other the son of a king without a kingdom, a frightened, bony little boy in a limp tweed cap.

And all of it inevitable.

But then Zack spoke. His voice cracked. "Want to go down?"

Eagle Foot looked at his father. Tendoy nodded. Eagle Foot picked up his cap and stood.

Lizzie said, "Go down where, Zack?"

"To the creek."

"Oh," she said. "Oh, fine!"

Yes, down to the creek where they'd played as little ones, then later as boys hunting the occasional garnet hurled down from the mountains, for the mussels that might hide a pearl. Down to the creek, down where two boys could talk like old men of a past they had once called a beginning.

*

At dawn, from the porch of the ranch house she watched. The Indians moved, a long line of them, dark against the quickening light behind the mountains, a classic frieze of figures repeated and repeated—horses and wheels and stragglers, horses and wheels and stragglers. Repeated and repeated as once again a people fled before selfishness and greed.

When the sun rose, they were gone; when the sun rose, that was the end of the halcyon days, the Days of the Indians when she and John were young and there was hope.

But see here: she and John Metlen now had all they'd hoped for, a ranch, a house in town and a hotel with a tower so tall it was the first and last thing a traveler saw in Grayling, Montana, and the word *METLEN*, high above, the name remembered.

Upstairs in his room among his jars and batteries, his wires and his prisms, was the fondest hope of all.

A shiver darted down her spine, and she hugged her shoulders.

Chapter
4

When a boy turns ten, a man wants to give him a .22 caliber rifle, if he can talk his wife into it. Women sometimes drag their heels and speak of accidents. Women don't like the idea of shooting; they don't like to see boys get older and become men because then they lose them.

A good many sissies have been made by women who won't let a boy have a gun.

"Do you want him to grow up to be a sissy?" What would she have to say about that?

"I'd rather see him be a sissy than get himself killed or kill somebody."

Oh, you would, would you. What was she trying to make of him, of her husband—a murderer?

"You see, what you have got to do, you have got to teach him how to handle a gun."

Stockton Township Public Library

Stockton, Illinois

"You say handle a gun. I don't want to hear handle a gun when a boy is ten years of age. It's when he's handling a gun that it happens."

Christ, a little bitty .22 rifle that only shoots shorts, not much more than a BB gun, so a kid can pop away at gophers and magpies. Everybody hates magpies. They hop around pretty as you please and when a calf or a little colt is born they pick out its eyes. They flap-flap-flap around up there till they spot a horse with a saddle sore, they sight it with those bright little beady eyes and they light and they sit right there on that horse and eat his living flesh. And she won't even let a boy shoot them.

But by God when a boy is twelve, he's going to have a rifle. He's going to learn to use it and he's going to be a real man.

John Metlen, however, offered no rifle to Zack when Zack was ten, and when Zack was twelve Lizzie made no objection to a Winchester rifle. She was wise enough to see the gift as a rite of passage, as important and mystical as Confirmation or the magic they do with boys in heathen lands.

She said only, "You're sure he wants one, John?"

"Any boy does."

The country was alive with game—deer, elk, moose. Not long ago one of Shineberger's hired hands got chased by a moose not a mile from the ranch house. Within an hour's ride on a good saddle horse you could spot lynx, bobcats, cougar, all of that. Farther up near the timberline were bear, black and brown, even a grizzly or two. A little higher, and there were mountain sheep and mountain goats. A goat head with shiny, needlelike horns was a good thing on a wall.

John made a rawhide scabbard for Zack's Winchester. You wouldn't believe it now, but once John was pretty good with his hands. He worked away in secret in the harness room in the barn and smiled to himself, wondering what Zack would make of that rawhide scabbard. It's hard to tell a son you love him. You don't tell him. You just say other things and do things, and hope he guesses.

Later on Zack might say, "My father made that scabbard. He surprised me with it."

You must speak carefully. You cannot say that a rifle arms a boy for the eternal confrontation between man and beast. A boy must sense that for himself.

Because school was still going on, they were back at the house in town when he gave Zack the Winchester. Maybe it would have been better to wait until they were at the ranch, because town didn't feel like a place for guns.

John had planned to present the rifle when Lizzie was gone, at a meeting of the DAR in Pioneer Hall where they sewed and ate sandwiches and pledged allegiance to the flag.

"Here's your rifle, Zack."

Zack held it, not expertly. "Thanks, Pa. Thanks a lot."

"I made the scabbard."

"It's a real beauty."

That's all Zack said. Proper words and polite, but Zack's eyes showed no surprise, no gratitude, not the excitement John expected when a boy held in his hands the power of the future. Damn it, no father has the right to expect gratitude from a boy who has been given only what he ought to have. Nevertheless, he was surprised to find he was a little hurt.

He would not, of course, speak to Lizzie of it. Zack hadn't meant to disappoint him and, because he was not yet a father, couldn't know how a father felt. A man should keep his trap shut. But John Metlen had a bad record about not telling things to his wife. So after dinner that same night he told her.

She was peeling an apple; she peeled apples carefully. He watched her hands. His own were stubby and broad and did what his brain directed, but hers struck him as having their own brains. Watching the silver blade lift a scarlet ribbon, he could not imagine a gun in her hands.

She liked to remove the entire peel in one piece; he watched as the thin peel coiled down into a little dish. What would her success augur for the future?

"There!" she said, and smiled. What disappointment had

she avoided? She placed peel and apple and knife and dish on the table beside her—the entire paraphernalia of divination.

"Well," he said, "Zack didn't think much of the rifle."

"He wasn't pleased, then?"

"He didn't say much more than thanks. No, he wasn't pleased."

"You must have had some feeling all along?"

"That he wouldn't be pleased? I can't imagine a boy's not wanting a gun."

"You can't, John? I wonder."

He spoke quietly, cautiously, as if a third person listened. "What do you wonder?"

She didn't speak at once, and then hesitantly. "I've often thought you didn't like guns. That you thought you ought to like them. Maybe most men have an instinct to kill. I don't think you have. I don't think Zack has."

He bit his lip. It was true. Long ago he'd taken a new gun to bed, but only because his father had given it to him.

Of the summer when John Metlen turned sixteen, he remembered the crawling feeling of loss and shame that came over him when he discovered in the attic his collection of birds' eggs. Like most of his friends in the little town where he boarded and went to school, he had given up childish hobbies the moment he was accepted by his peers. And by this time he saw that every delicately blown shell was emptied of a song.

There was one boy in town who had not given up his hobby, because he had no friends, or had no friends because he had not given it up. His name was David Lubin and he played the piano, which is a thing usually done by your mother or your aunt. He was of fragile build, they called it scrawny, and his eyes were careful not to meet anyone's. John remembered the sound of his piano tinkling across from the lot where, if they couldn't muster enough of the fellows for more than one base, the boys played One-old-cat. They did not include David Lubin; they couldn't see him with a ball or bat.

David Lubin's mother made dresses for ladies.

"She's awfully good with her hands," he'd heard his mother remark to another woman. "Isn't it a shame."

John figured that the shame wasn't that there wasn't a Mr. Lubin but the reason there wasn't a Mr. Lubin.

Mrs. Lubin had often smiled at him on the street when he was with some friends; he felt the smile was particularly for him. He knew her only as a large, anxious woman with a bit of fur around her neck. He felt that one of these days—he hoped when he was alone—she was going to speak to him. And she did.

Never before had he seen her so close; the fur around her neck was a little narrow animal that bit its own tail to stay on.

"Well, now," she said, "if it isn't young John Metlen!" She stepped back to see him from another distance. "I saw your mother on the street yesterday."

John had found that when older people stop you on the street, they want something.

"You know," Mrs. Lubin said, "I thought it might be nice if you came to our house sometime, and had a nice cup of chocolate."

He couldn't imagine it. His mouth dried up and his tongue failed. John Metlen had never been blessed with guile. Every possible excuse fled. He got words out. "That would be fine, sometime," he said, grateful for the elusive word. "Real nice."

She touched her lips with two fingers, and frowned, and then she struck. "How about tomorrow, right after school." It was not a question.

He thought nobody but the Lubins ever knew of his visit. Had a friend asked him why he went there, he would have lied, said something about an errand for his mother. He wasn't sure why he'd gone, but it wasn't really that she'd trapped him. It had something to do with Mrs. Lubin's having exposed her naked heart.

So he knocked on the door. Mrs. Lubin opened it; the doorway led into no entrance hall. No hatrack, no coat tree, no umbrella stand, no mirror where you can try on a few faces before you go in. He had looked directly across a small room to a sewing machine that she used for her business, and to a piano where David sat playing, not a square piano made of rosewood like those in the houses where he went, but an old black upright they make for people who must settle for close quarters and second best.

"Why, John Metlen!" Mrs. Lubin cried to him, and turned her head. "David, it's John Metlen." Exactly as if she wasn't expecting him. David turned, and their eyes met. Now he must act as if he had come to surprise, and by choice.

"Do you like your teachers at the school?" Mrs. Lubin asked.

His mind fled over his teachers, scurried like a rat searching for some shiny piece to replace something stolen. He could think of nothing but a pocket comb a teacher carried in his breast pocket.

"Mr. Mann's all right," he said.

"Mr. Mann," Mrs. Lubin said, and nodded, and touched her lips. "David, do you like Mr. Mann?"

"Yes, he's all right," David said.

"There must be other fine teachers at the school," Mrs. Lubin said, her warm smile certainly meant for them who might be overlooked. "I've heard it's one of the best schools in the state. Oh, I'm sure there are other fine teachers."

"Some of them are all right," John said.

She leaned to him, her eyes serious. "Just what is it you're studying, John?"

His mind fled again. "History."

"Oh-ho!" she said. "And our own California history, I expect. A truly interesting history."

He was afraid she was going to speak of his grandfather, and of gold. "And English and geometry," he said.

"Geometry," she said, and shook her head. "I'm afraid I missed geometry."

David spoke suddenly, swiveling around on the piano stool. "Is geometry all right?" David was smiling, and spoke like a bantering grown-up. "Is geometry all right, John?"

For a second John missed the sarcasm and thought only, What a funny question, but then it washed over him that David Lubin was mocking him. In mocking, David let him know that he'd known nothing of his mother's meeting with John on the street, didn't know John was coming, didn't want him to come, and was supposed to believe that John had come to be a friend.

But David was no fool. David knew the social order on the playground and in the halls of the high school. And David had accepted that order, every bit of it, and dismissed it as a cripple dismisses his clubfoot—simply a part of him.

What shame David must have felt that his mother had exposed them both in appealing to John for what could not be granted in that town, in that day, or in any town, in any day. Sheep steer clear of goats.

"David?" Mrs. Lubin was saying. "I thought you too were taking geometry. Why, I'm sure you are."

Next year the Lubins moved away. Passing that house where he'd been so desperate a prisoner, John wished he'd offered his hand in friendship. He still did. Maybe if he had, things would have been different for them. And for John Metlen.

Chapter
5

Grayling was no dismal Gopher Prairie in 1913. Books in the gray stone Carnegie library were read. True, men talked about the weather, the hay crop, the price of beef and whether a man had got his deer that fall; spittoons were handy in saloons and bars, in the Pheasant and the Smoke House and the Owl, but it was beginning to dawn on guests that gentlemen didn't spit into the spittoons in the Metlen Hotel. Cigars were giving way to cigarettes— Mecca, Fatima, Camel. More than one lady was known to smoke.

People from Grayling felt but reasonable excitement when they registered at the Palmer House in Chicago or the new Palace in San Francisco. A few citizens had even laid eyes on the Flatiron Building and reported that all that was said was true, that it did indeed resemble a flatiron, and that it was truly constructed of iron, and so shaped that if you walked too quickly around the corner of it, your hat blew off.

Many women admired the craft of Poiret and put their hands on Butterick patterns that did him justice. Men swore by Hart, Schaffner & Marx and on French, Shriner & Urner. The luster of the Copper Kings spread down from Butte to the north, sharp, clever, unscrupulous men whose daughters had married into nobility and things like that.

There had recently appeared in Grayling from Salt Lake City a man with easy manners and a fat wallet. His wife was a smart-looking woman with that clear, radiant complexion you see around Salt Lake City—something about the air, some believed, or the clean living that Mormons are said to practice. A boy and a girl about Zack Metlen's age then appeared.

The man bought up many small farms in the foothills; he talked to the government about range rights. Shortly afterward, ten thousand head of sheep arrived, herded up from the south by Basques.

And then the man built his house.

The man was blatantly competitive; word was that he'd deliberately built his house to be bigger than Martin Connard's. It was far bigger than John Metlen's house in town, and of a style called Dutch Colonial; benches were built into the porch on either side of the thick front door, where a massive knocker gleamed. The house was chalk white with a green shake roof and green blinds at every window. Those who got themselves inside claimed sixteen rooms and a laundry chute down which dirty clothes could be released. The lawn was wide and deep and green, and the man had brought into it full-grown trees set in place by a derrick. They might have begun there fifty years before as saplings.

Although you could not have asked for a pleasanter, more jovial man, quick to smile and take your hand and shake it, he was thought perhaps not to be sincere; that once he greeted you, you fled his mind. It seemed excessive that his wife dressed for supper. They were, in short, the kind of people you hope and rather expect to go broke suddenly, to vanish so quickly they leave behind a trilling vacuum. And a few years later, that is just what happened. But you ask few questions of a man who has a Peerless and a Pierce-Arrow in his garage, not many questions of a woman with long strings of pearls.

In 1913 they gave a party, not for themselves, not for their old friends or new friends, but for young people. Nobody in Grayling had ever heard of making such a fuss over children. The guest of honor was to be young Harry Connard, who had just finished with that school over there in Seattle. A band was to come down from Butte. The staff of the Sugar Bowl Café had been engaged to cook and wait on the young people. Flowers came up from the south on the Union Pacific. The nodding local lilacs would not do.

The very word "party" is brief, ephemeral and frivolous. A party is done before the sun comes up. What remains but crumpled napkins, wilting flowers and stains? But entire forests are devastated for wood pulp for paper to describe the gowns and to list the invited guests. It's clear in black on white who counts and who does not. Who is in, who is out. Men have shot themselves; women have swallowed poison.

Not everybody in Grayling counted. John Metlen ticked off some thirty sons and daughters who'd be present, and there'd be young people from the mansions on Park Street in Butte. The sons and daughters of the Old Families in Grayling were at the center of it, the sons and daughters of those who, like John Metlen, had come early, whose grandfathers' enlarged photographs hung in oval frames downtown in Pioneer Hall between the flags of the United States and the state of Montana; those faces as the years passed acquired a patina of sanctity. But those alone would make too small a party, and in these last years it was perceived that little harm comes from shaking hands with a butcher. Time plays funny tricks: the Armours and the Swifts and the Cudahays and the Wilsons were all butchers, but their grandsons didn't hear the scream of hogs. The sons and daughters of Grayling's doctors would be there, and those of the dentists. To exclude the undertaker's son might prove self-defeating, and after all, somebody has got to bury you. All those who would attend were "up and coming," a current phrase—likely to amount to something, and a hostess too selective would find scant use for flat silver for twenty.

The pawnbroker's daughter was not included. Her father did his business in the front room of his house on Kentucky Avenue, never a good address because it bordered the Cabbage Patch. The windows were quite like a store's; across them the man at night pulled folding steel shutters and he locked them and so defended rings and guitars and mandolins, garnet brooches and elks' teeth set in golden gums. He and the woman who was his wife lived in basement rooms, slept there, it is supposed, and cooked and planned. Some wondered why people who must be rich lived this way. You know what it is if you have to pawn something—they turn around and sell it for five times what you owed them. The daughter walked alone to school, where she was said to get very high marks.

A Miss Ruby Finch, raven-haired, quick of smile, was not bidden; she was wildly popular with the football boys on those many occasions when they carried her off into the bushes behind Graymont Park. She was not so attended in the halls of the high school; she gave way when her betters passed, and she drank alone at the bubbler. She got no invitation.

Nor, so it seemed, did Zack Metlen.

"It's only a party," Lizzie said quietly. "It doesn't really matter."

It was a party in early June to welcome back young Harry Connard. You'd think these new people in town would know by now that a party for a Connard meant an invitation for a Metlen. Had the invitation been lost? An envelope can slip through cracks, fly out a window, stick to the bottom of a sack. The invitation might have fluttered to the floor and never been mailed; any moment now the telephone might ring, and an apology be heard. Dozens, hundreds of things happen to envelopes.

"Who are these people, anyway?" John asked, knowing very well who they were.

"Well, you know where they live. I haven't met her yet. They're gone a lot."

Would they be gone if he went to their big new house and knocked on the door and said, "I am John Metlen and I want to know if you sent my son an invitation because if you did it seems to be lost"?

But he did not do this, because he was afraid the man or the woman would stand there and say to him, "No, we did not send your son an invitation."

Maybe it was Lizzie's fault for not making friends with the woman. But no. The fact was, Zack wasn't popular. Not since Tendoy's boy had Zack had a special friend, although John had thought he'd find one as soon as they had moved into town for the winter. Then there'd be bicycles in the yard and overshoes at the back door and Lizzie fussing over wet caps and mittens. But that did not happen. John was sure that Zack was pleasant to the children at school, because Zack was a pleasant child, and fixed his eyes intently on you when you spoke; he was polite to teachers, because they stopped his father on the street and told him so. But no boys hollered for Zack from the pavement in front of the house in town, and Zack had never asked a boy out to the ranch in the summertime. Zack was never with the others, not on the ballfield, not in the snake dance after a game, not with the fellows who slouched outside the Pheasant poolroom, never with a cigarette in his mouth that John would have been glad to catch him with and then deliver a lecture about but explaining how every cigarette was a nail in your coffin. Instead, Zack stayed in the school lab as long as they'd let him, and then he was in his room.

He was, John thought, in hiding.

How could this have happened? John stared at himself in the mirror and pulled the razor across his face and remembered how it was to leap up the steps of a house where you were wanted, to look across the room to the girls waiting in their party dresses, to be there when the fiddles tuned up for the grand march. Ah, but he had loved to dance. He couldn't share his little anguish about Zack with Lizzie, because a mother grieves, wishes popularity for her son, too. But now for days he'd been afraid to reach out and to touch Zack, afraid to punch him on the arm as men do, afraid Zack would see the gesture for what it was—pity for a boy who was not chosen. Christ—and how pity does pick at scabs and keep wounds raw. But by God, this night, about the time the fiddles tuned up in that big new white house, he was going right up there into Zack's room and he was going to—

Going to what? To see if Zack was all right? Yes, and more. Tongue thick in his dry mouth, he was going to say, "Zack, I love you."

*

That evening Zack said, "Excuse me, Mum? Pa?" Zack rose from his chair and turned and climbed the stairs. John noted the plate he'd left. But Zack never ate much. John had never seen him tear into a steak or wolf down a pie. When he heard footsteps above him, John frowned and thought of going up at once.

Zack, however, would not welcome him. A man's humiliation is as private as a man's balls.

So time fell away, the clock in the courthouse struck seven; its clear brass waves scudded over the town, over the hospital, over the tall sagebrush and the shacks in the Cabbage Patch where the sidewalks ended. At eight the sun slipped behind the Rockies; the afterglow shimmered over the sudden silence. Then the Union Pacific whistled for the trestle north of town; there would be passengers on board from Butte, young people, and a chaperon or two.

The party would begin at nine. When it ended, an elect of young people would understand the witchery of midnight; when the courthouse struck twelve, they would no longer be boys and girls but young men and women poised, like the clock's iron hands, at the apex of time, all of them about to receive precious new rights and privileges. Since the Metlen house was at the far end of the long street, Zack need not suffer the festive little groups that gathered to the music and to the punch bowl honoring young Harry Connard. . . .

This painful thought had not yet dissipated when up the quiet street, purring, moved an automobile, a double-cowled twin-six Packard phaeton with room for seven—a long, low, golden magnificence. John thought he knew every important car for forty miles around, but this one was gleaming new and strange to him. And lively it was with young men dressed in striped blazers, boaters and white flannel trousers.

The driver of the machine could hardly be nineteen; to allow a boy of that age to drive such a car was obscene. It was too early a taste of what was to be his inheritance; but that boy's real inheritance was the company of his lordlike friends.

That boy was young Harry Connard.

His appearance struck John as portentous: this young man was the last young man he would have wished to look upon. This young man possessed those very qualities of which he was envious for Zack—he was horribly at ease in Zion. He drove with one hand on the wheel. The other hand and arm lay along the quilted glove leather of the front seat, starched white shirt cuff peeking out just so from the sleeve of his blazer. That arm was possessive; clearly Grayling was hardly big enough for him. Now he was the returning prince. John felt pursued. Hadn't the car slowed perceptibly as it approached, and then passed, the house? Did he imagine it?

Of course he did. For that young man sitting there with his courtiers had everything he wished and no thought at all of Zack Metlen, who was nothing and had nothing a Connard wanted.

John turned and climbed the stairs. He would speak as a friend to Zack, not as a father. And as a friend, respecting privacy, he knocked at Zack's door upstairs.

Zack called out at once, "Come in."

John had always been uneasy at the door of that room. It was not what a boy's room should be. No high school banner was tacked to the wall, no Kodak snapshots of fellows arm in arm, no fishing gear, no banjo, no comfortable clutter. For friends, Zack had substituted the stuff of a junk shop, an uncomfortable clutter—dry cells, ammeters, Leyden jars.

"Thought I'd look in a minute, Zack."

Lizzie had missed the point in saying that the party didn't matter. Of course the party didn't matter. Living was more than a dance card and a dish of sherbet. But a party made clear who was accepted and who was not. What safety a man knows is only in the tribe. The ostracized man is lost. He has no protector. After the hunt he's left with only the stripped carcass.

Zack stood beside a heavy mission oak table he'd retrieved from the basement. It supported three early wall telephones abandoned downtown after the telephone company had sold their owners a bill of goods: the latest telephones were movable. You sat down to use them.

John was not yet comfortable with a telephone. When he was about to talk into one a frog crept into his throat and he pressed his palm against the mouthpiece so his cough wouldn't be heard. A telephone required that you speak with your best voice, since the other end couldn't see you and might take advantage of what it heard as weakness or illness. He thought no one he knew, except Zack, understood how telephones worked. It had been explained, but not to his satisfaction. Something to do with carbon. Often he had looked overhead at the wires on poles beside the road to Butte, marveling that they could accommodate so many voices raised in sorrow, anger, joy; strangest of all, each sounding like its speaker. He wondered as he wondered at the moon that rose huge and grew smaller as it climbed and then tagged along beside you as you sat in a train coach or drove a car.

He moved and stood near Zack. Beside the boy was an open ledger, scrawled with words and figures. Whatever Zack was doing, it was important enough to record. "I don't want to interrupt," he said, as a friend might who knew perfectly well he was interrupting and went right ahead and did it.

"You're not. I'm glad you came in."

John glanced at the cold, metallic clutter on the table. "I can't make sense of telephones."

"They're pretty simple, Pa."

"Come on, Zack!" But proud that Zack understood.

"Simple when you understand the principle."

Principles, John thought. If only a man understood the principles.

"Here, Pa. Look here." John moved closer, closer than he'd stood to Zack for a long time, so close that he was suddenly aware of the odor of Zack's skin—surely a Metlen odor, but not exactly his own or he wouldn't have been aware of it, and John felt suddenly shy at having approached so close. "Look, Pa. This is a simple magneto. When this coil turns between the opposite poles of this magnet, you get a current. All right?"

"All right what?" John asked.

"That's the principle. You get an electric current."

And what did you get, John wondered, when a man turns between opposite poles? You got something. And then as if Zack had read his thoughts, Zack said quietly, "And nobody knows what it is, Pa. Just that it's there and everywhere, and it can do anything. Like God."

The word shocked John. He'd never before heard that word on the lips of a young person except in profanity. He could not remember hearing that word on the lips of an old person except in profanity or in a church when the word was dropped from the pulpit. He couldn't decide whether his embarrassment at hearing the word was that it stood for an idea so patently ridiculous, or whether he felt an atavistic reluctance to speak or hear spoken the Ineffable Name.

Zack had spoken the name not in profanity but as a pagan who had invoked the god, and flattered the god as one who could do anything, and then presented a petition. In presenting it, Zack was another young David Lubin so many years ago when that young fellow practiced his interminable scales on the piano while outside the others shouted and played ball in the vast afternoon. How like Zack and all the others he was, in whatever small rooms, who desperately hoped and dreamed imperial dreams to compensate for their rejection by those who gathered at the punch bowl.

But Zack was looking directly into his father's eyes, and when he spoke it might have been John's own voice. "I'm not like them, Pa. They're not my speed."

Chapter
6

For Chief Tendoy and his people, the trip to the sere, dusty flats of southern Idaho was a funeral march; the streams along the way stank of alkali. But another dirge was about to sound.

The halcyon days were running out—and what good days they were. Everything was settled, everything was known and doubt was at rest. The last pictures worth a critic's notice had all been painted; the tubes, as Kipling put it, were twisted and dried. In France a few self-styled artists were daubing gaudy colors on canvas like excited children, and quite rightly they were labeled Wild Beasts. There was small place in those good days for wild beasts.

Music was settled in 1911 with the death of Mahler—what is left for the human voice after _Kindertotenlieder_? After Rodin's _Nijinsky_, what is there left for stone? All that was good and true and lasting had just now been pressed on fine onionskin paper between the dark green covers of the *Britannica,* the masterwork of the finest minds. Even God was defined there in all His guises and manifestations. It was clear that God was most active and effective in Christian communities to whom He had wisely given ascendancy over other communities. It was the duty of the Christian to rule, to police, and to succor.

In those halcyon days all national boundaries had been defined and drawn, sanctioned by solemn treaty and the Divine Right of Kings. War was now unthinkable; the lion had laid himself down with the lamb, and small disputes might be arbitrated by the British on whose empire the sun would never set.

The *Grayling Examiner* was unaware that anything ominous was afoot. Instead, it reported that the Ed Coles had motored to Butte in their handsome new Paige. The Coles intended to do some shopping; to spare the feelings of the local dentists, it was not written that the Coles meant to have their teeth looked into. The Coles rightly assumed that the cleverest dentists settled in the larger communities, where life, too, was larger.

It was not noted that the Archduke Franz Ferdinand had decided to motor over to Sarajevo in his handsome new Austro-Daimler.

Across the Continental Divide in the Salmon River country—according to the *Examiner*—a party of four, including a woman, had successfully run the rapids down the River of No Return on a raft constructed by themselves. Photographs accompanied the piece, one of them of the woman in trousers and high laced boots, holding up a big trout.

"The recent discovery of the Salmon River by Eastern dudes is bound to add to that locality's prosperity, and to benefit our sister city of Salmon." Cynical readers might wonder what the Eastern dudes made of the high, shaky old iron bridge that spanned the Salmon River in the sister city.

Odd facts and nuggets of advice evened up the columns.

Baking soda serves as an excellent dentifrice. Wood screws go in easier if first rubbed across a bar of softened soap. Tomatoes were once thought to be poisonous. Bloodstains must be soaked in cold—never hot—water.

". . . has returned from Seattle. Young Connard has now completed his first year at the University of Washington. Attaboy, Harry!"

Not noted in the *Examiner:* days later young Harry Connard smashed up his new yellow Mercer Raceabout on the S-curve beside the river mouth at Graymont Park. A young woman passenger in the automobile was removed to the hospital. When she regained consciousness, she was handed a paper, and she signed it; she was rewarded with a sum of money. Pretty expensive wild oats, but some felt that old Connard guessed that young Harry had learned a good lesson.

The automobile was left for dead. Next morning it was viewed for some time by many who had eaten hurried breakfasts; then two men came from the Ford Garage with a tow truck; the sun played on the brass fittings. Zachary Metlen made a deal with the garage for the battery and the generator and added them to his collection of junk. John Metlen kept his mouth shut, but he didn't like Zack's using young Harry's leavings.

"The Grayling Illumination and Power Company has taken delivery of a new hundred-thousand-watt generator." A hundred thousand watts! No matter what a watt was, that was impressive, but John Metlen did not cry out, Attaboy, Connard.

Except for the bank, the power company was Connard's most successful enterprise. The man, someone had remarked, even owned light and darkness. The power company was an especially sore point with John Metlen. He, too, might have invested in the dam in the river, but he had not had the money—he had already built his hotel, had even had to borrow money from the bank to complete it.

And for some years the hotel made money, and John had been so prompt at paying back the principal and the interest that it made him feel good. Yes, he'd had to use more than capital to build his hotel, and borrow from Connard's bank, but that's what banks are for. You hire money from them to make money. Otherwise there wouldn't be any banks, wouldn't be any Connard.

But now the hotel was in the red—a reproach to a fellow who should have realized from the beginning that all he knew was ranching. All the old crowd had acquired other strings to their bows—a hardware store, business blocks, a brickworks, a stone quarry. Shineberger had considered a brewery; his grandfather had owned one in the Old Country. But John had known nothing of hotels. Some might believe he'd been public-spirited in building his hotel. Some might say he wanted his hotel to rival Connard's bank—a fellow will pick a rival, and try to beat him. A rival is a spur.

In fact, he had built his hotel because of a voice inside his head.

Build a hotel.

And then, *Build it high, with a tower.*

And finally, *Write your name on it. METLEN.*

*

When they heard what had happened to the yellow Mercer Raceabout, John said, "Thank God it wasn't Zack. He could have been killed."

"You're scaring yourself," Lizzie said, "so when you get through you can feel good. It couldn't have been Zack."

No, it couldn't have been Zack. Whatever might threaten Zack, it wasn't high speeds and flashy cars. Zack was cautious. There again he was not like his father. Because watching him grow, John had observed that they were different, son and father. John took chances and only afterward perceived what he had done; he was impetuous. He jumped ahead. So far he had always landed on thick ice—well, most of the time he had. Zack traveled deliberately and in one direction; he tested as he went.

And John's attention flew about and was easily distracted;

a scent could do it, a color, Lizzie's quiet voice. Zack's was a glacier, moving slowly, inexorably, down a narrow draw. John liked and needed to exchange ideas; he felt easier, knowing what the other fellow thought. Zack seldom expressed an opinion.

But look here.

John had noticed that when a boy resembles his father, they oftentimes lock horns, like a young buck and an old buck who claim the same mountain meadow. Well, he and Zack had never done that. Not once had they faced each other in rage and fear, and they never would, by God. Because in that, at least, they were dead alike. They were not horn-lockers.

In the past year, his last in high school, Zack had been shaving, although his beard was no more than peach fuzz. Never had John said to him, "Just put some cream on your face and let the cat lick it off."

For that is what John's uncle had said to him. His uncle was a big man with a mustache so formidable he combed it; he had fought in the Civil War and had a sword; he was a hero, the family said, and whenever he arrived there was a good deal of talk about him before he came.

His uncle and the rest of them who hung around thought it comical that a boy should dare aspire to be a man—that in shaving the down he now stood as a man, who smoked, who chewed, who married a woman and went to bed with her. A man stayed up all night if he liked, slept in his underwear, made money and saved it or spent it on what he wanted.

But standing in the broad door of the long log barn, the apricot sunlight slanting into his eyes, standing with a son who had shaved for months, John wondered if it hadn't been uneasiness that had prompted his uncle the hero to taunt him. Because the moment a boy became a man, his father and uncle and all the rest of them became the ones who'd soon need the arm or the hand of this boy who had dared to use a razor. Before you could blink an eye, the years had blown ahead of you like tumbleweeds, and no fence to stop them. If a son was like you, he would stand so close he'd be there when you needed him. If your son was like you, he would take your place when the time came, just as John had thought to stand by his father, and would have too, had he been chosen.

John thought Zack would not. And to Lizzie he said, "What will become of the ranch, Lizzie?"

She didn't speak at once; he saw that she'd wondered, too. "John—I think if we'd had a daughter, you'd never have thought she'd take over. Why should a man be trapped because he's a man?"

Trapped?

She went on, "You wouldn't want him tied here because he loves you, or out of duty, or because he was afraid he couldn't make it on his own. As for the ranch, we're not dead yet."

Trapped? John wondered if the ranch hadn't trapped *him*. Now that she spoke of being dead, wasn't life itself a trap, and everybody struggling to get out? Was that the point of death—to get out? The foolish poet in him remarked that losing a son was a little like death, and for no other reason than a small red magnet.

Chapter
7

The *Examiner* printed news of the county, noting that the Latest Out Mining Company had sunk two new shafts; state news appeared, should it concern the county or Grayling— new legislation in Helena about range or water rights or the danger of hoof and mouth disease. Tax proposals were watched.

National news was left to the *Miner* in Butte. In Butte were more than fifty thousand people; among so many, some were bound to have a more than casual interest in the larger United States. Sometimes the *Miner* pulled out all the stops, looked abroad and told sad stories of the death of kings, but such foreign items appeared as features, showing that not one among us is immune to pain and heartbreak; that it is better to be an American because of the way Americans are. The outbreak of war in Europe was not surprising to those who considered Europe; the Balkan countries bickered, stole property, had to return it, turned on their neighbors. The Turks were about done. Nobody had ever known one. The Rumanians were fine sheepherders; they worked for less because they weren't used to money. They didn't drink too much, and then usually wine. In the Old Country they let the sheep come in the house with them.

The war over there was good for business over here. Cattle prices were looking up. The French and the rest of them needed beef and hides for boots and saddles; because they were fighting they couldn't raise their own. Besides, cows are as likely to get shot as anybody else.

That wasn't going to happen over here, because we were neutral, a good thing to be. But recently whispers told of factories that were tooling up back East, in places like Massachusetts and the White Mountains. These factories were getting ready to manufacture olive-drab woolens, the kind only American soldiers wore. It looked like the owners were up to something. Or somebody was.

It was hard to believe the Germans could be so foolish as to sink the *Lusitania:* an English ship and unarmed and Americans on board. At first people thought maybe there really weren't any Americans on board. Nobody in Grayling, and nobody anyone had heard of, had received a death notice, and the whispers about the factories came to mind.

But it was true. Americans had gone down. It's hard at first to feel much about people you don't know, even Americans; it takes some time to get worked up. But they did know about one man who'd sunk to his watery grave. His name was Elbert Hubbard. He was known far and wide by those who took stock in reading. He wrote an essay called "A Message to Garcia" about the value of fidelity and enterprise; businessmen handed it around to their employees to make them better and more faithful. But most of all Hubbard was known for his *Scrapbook.* That was a collection of poems and sayings that showed you what to think and how to be, what to feel and what to put into your rooms. Printed on good heavy paper, it was a nice book to lay on a table; a guest left alone in the room might go over and read it.

Such a ruckus there was over the *Lusitania.* The Germans promised they wouldn't torpedo anybody without warning, and not if there were any Americans on board; but they broke the promise, and then it turned out from a telegram that the Germans had promised the Mexicans if they'd declare war on the United States the Germans would give them back Texas and California and everything. That was pretty close to home, so the President declared war.

The Great War was not popular around Grayling. It was hard to look at the Rocky Mountains and believe in the Rape of Belgium. The Germans in Grayling and around there were just like anybody else, and as for the Anheuser-Busches, the Pabsts, and the Schlitzes—they were responsible for many a high old time at picnics and on the Fourth; you can't get much more American than that.

The war was not popular among many whose sons smiled out from recent high school photographs on the upright piano.

But as for the sons themselves, it was sometimes different. As young beasts, they felt the tug, as regular as the tide, that pulls every twenty years or so. The old, important men in the land know this, and find it not hard to convince the young men that the real purpose of your real man is to kill an enemy. Oh, many young men believe that the battleground is the place to be and not here where they're stuck. A young man's sick of raincloud under raincloud hanging over Puget Sound, of the flat Kansas horizon, of the dull monotonous rote of the Atlantic against a granite coast. All empty and predictable. Tomorrow will become another yesterday, the same meat on the table, the same thing certain to be said. A fellow wasn't born just for that. Nothing is so unwelcoming as the same old bed.

The winter had been cold, but there was no snow. Nothing looked like the Christmas cards, and the new Flexible Flyers still leaned in the halls. But paths didn't have to be shoveled, sidewalks cleared, icy drifts cut away from the garage door. The fanciful, who regularly saw human faces in the grain and knots of wood, who watched monsters moving through the skies, missed the sheltering snow beneath which the earth could be said to sleep. Without that coverlet the earth looked dead, the dry grass but a pall. Each year when the snow in the high mountains melted in the spring and the first little rivulets ran down and around the roots of the sagebrush, the bluebells sprang up and the little gray birds darted about; from cirques and slopes the melting snow found the little creeks and swelled the rivers, and the earth stirred and woke.

But that year, in the mountains, there was little snow.

In April the sunlight continued thin and grudging. From the classrooms at the university one could see, high on the flank of a brown hill, a dozen wild horses wandering, but the sight of them was no less bleak than the books laid open on the desks.

Its head end, the pronephros, survives only for a short period of time during embryonic development and is represented by convoluted ciliated tubules that open into the coelom at one end and form archinephric ducts at the other end.

. . . and somewhere the boys are marching.

What in the world was this university doing out there on the edge of nothing and why had anybody ever enrolled there. Then at last the girls, who have an eye for such things, reported crocuses on the south side of Main Hall. Oh, how the sudden appearance of a bit of color will lift the spirits even of those who have failed the midyear examinations, who have been ready, except for parents, to throw in the towel, and to hightail it.

But now an even wilder wind roared out of the north, and the crocuses were seen as cheats.

The wind was at its height when Wilson declared war.

Who in the Junior Class first cried the call to arms? Maybe it was he who had stood on the broad porch of the Kappa

House with her whom he considered his sweetheart, and who still held the two-pound box of Whitman's chocolates he'd charged to his hazardous account at the Student Store.

He had come to her hoping to make her sit up and take notice.

"I've decided to go to war," he said. Just what the first move was, in going to war, he wasn't sure, but so strong and simple a statement as his brushed all doubt aside.

And this is what she said. "Silly."

Silly!

"I mean it, Gladys."

"You men," she said.

"Silly to be a man?"

"Oh, my friend Marjorie Bacon I was telling you about, she lives back there in Buffalo, I told you, called me up on the telephone long-distance if you please. Oh, I guess it was Tuesday, because we had lamb. She said her beau joined up last week. She said joined the colors. Her voice was just as clear as a bell."

You could have knocked him over with a feather. How could this girl, this female, speak of the speaking voice of Marjorie Bacon when he was about to put his life on the line? It was clear by this speech of hers that she was daring him to equal Marjorie Bacon's beau. A woman has no conception of a man's responsibilities, how he's the one who always has to buy everything and has to go to war. She had, in fact, forced him into what he had not yet decided upon, and very likely she might regret for the rest of her natural life what she'd forced him into. And later, maybe, when she looked over her old dance programs she'd remember and be ashamed of herself.

In any event, it was not likely that the Dean of Men would expect a man to hang around and take examinations in June with democracy at stake. When they got back from Over There, the examinations would very likely be forgiven them and they'd move on to be seniors.

The Class of '17 at the University of Montana is remembered for its astonishing patriotism, and by the construction, a few years later, of a brick fountain with a stone lion's head that spat a faltering stream of water into a fluted basin high enough for a horse to drink from. The patriots' names were engraved on polished granite, and to those among them who had died at Ypres, a star was granted.

*

Of those young men John said, "They're like sheep following a bellwether."

All that Zack's letter had said was that he was coming home.

Neither of them knew what to make of it.

Both of them wished one thing and feared another. John had been thinking that the war might end before Zack was graduated. They were not yet drafting upperclassmen. But the factories were still turning out Sam Brownes and puttees, and it was a long shot from being over Over There. They still needed horses for the cavalry and beef for the doughboys. So he had the right to hope that what Zack had in mind was returning to the ranch, where even the government knew that he was needed, if he would just ask. John had lost three hired hands to the army. A man can't do it all alone. Martin Connard had seen to it that young Harry wasn't going. In the bars they said he was needed at the bank. Then they winked.

Lizzie said, "Knowing Zack, I don't think he thinks the way the others do. Whatever that is. I think that Zack thinks otherwise. Furthermore, as a boy he didn't want that rifle. I don't think he'll go."

John was grateful to her because of the way she marshaled facts and saw behind things. If she was right—and he honestly couldn't remember when she had been wrong—then what a paradox, that the war was giving Zack back to them. And Zack could settle into the ranch routine knowing full well that as far as the war was concerned, the fields were as important as the trenches. Didn't they say an army traveled on its stomach? But some grand gesture must be made and Zack be rewarded. John knew exactly what that reward must be.

The timing was providential. The Mountain States Automobile Show had just opened in Butte in the Armory, where the National Guard hung out. There, two years before, he had bought his Packard to replace the old Lozier he'd jacked up and stored in the carriage house. A fine car, the Packard, but an old man's car. The King of Cars this year was a Locomobile phaeton that they'd moved into the lobby of the Hotel Thornton and roped off with plush. Not an old man's car.

Lizzie showed little enthusiasm. "I imagine it's very expensive."

He had a hunch it wasn't the expense that bothered her, but the principle—she would look on the car as a bribe, when it was simply a gift from a grateful father. His son would have the best of a young man's dreams. What Lizzie—maybe any woman—would not understand was that the automobile had succeeded the horse in a man's world as an extension of his very self. It was the automobile that now appeared in a man's dreams, came to the rescue, carried away the prize. Loftiest of all cars was the Locomobile.

"Suppose you wait," Lizzie said, "and see what he's got to say?"

But John wasn't very good at waiting. On the train to Butte he tortured himself with the possibility that somebody else had bought the car. Earlier he had considered calling the Thornton Hotel—that might have saved him the trip. But if he knew the truth, he could no longer hope. Surely Divine Providence, observing him board the train, could not be so heartless as to snatch that car from him.

And it was still there!

He drove it away from the hotel at dusk, passed out of Butte along Park Street where the Copper Kings lived and into the flatlands where arsenic-heavy smoke from the smelters had killed almost every living green thing; far to his left a chain of ragged hills flowed along like a serpent's spine.

*

He was proud driving the great tan car in from the ranch to meet Zack. He didn't cross the Union Pacific tracks but parked the car near the south platform where the train would conceal it. The brute magnificence of the machine would show when the train drew away.

Then on foot he crossed the tracks to his hotel. It was satisfying to hear the good-natured noise and voices in the bar; friends and acquaintances smiled and made way. As he approached the bar, one clapped him on the shoulder.

"John, old man, hear your boy's joining up."

John smiled uncomfortably and shrugged; later, Ed Rife could make of it what he would.

"But there's a lot of slackers out there, John." And Ed Rife waved an arm to "out there" where the slackers cowered.

How quickly a young man—a boy—who believed in something else became a slacker when the brass sounded. How many of them knew why they were off to war? One fact was certain and always had been: somebody profited. Somebody profited in a room apart who never heard the screams of wounded men or watched a youngster die. For what? For Liberty? For the Pursuit of Profit?

By God, he could not imagine an abstraction for which a father would be willing to have his own son risk his life.

Ed Rife was saying, "We'll give the Heinies hell."

We. Rife had sat out the Spanish War in his hardware store. How would this patriot greet him at the bar when he found out that Zack would spend the war on the ranch: branding, dehorning, irrigating, haying? Why, Rife would move away down the bar from the man who owned it but had a son who was a slacker.

"Got business to attend to," John said, and escaped.

He walked a little later to the depot. In a sky so vast as that above Grayling there was a lot of room, and yet a cloud hid the sun. The railroad maintained the grounds around the depot; a raked gravel path meandered through some cottonwoods, their leaves just unfolding. Lizzie would say the leaves resembled green butterflies. Cobblestones spelling out "Grayling" and so placed that passengers could read them were freshly whitewashed. Two benches cast in concrete marked the north and south boundaries of the tiny park. There a man might rest or unwrap a sandwich and eat it. No man ever did.

John noticed two new flowerbeds, carefully prepared and showing recent raking, though not one green thing had yet appeared. Bordered with whitewashed stones, they resembled new-made graves. He looked away and up at the sky again. Lord knows, Grayling was a pretty small place in the scheme of things, and he himself not a big man.

He thought he could feel underground waves minutes before the black face of the locomotive appeared far down the line; he thought he heard a whining in the rails. The usual scattering of men had gathered to see the train pull in, though since the war there was little enough to watch. Those who were going to leave Grayling had pretty much left; the ranks had thinned of those who were likely to arrive. When the proud churning of the pistons stopped and the black porter jumped down with his little stool, a drummer got off with his sample case, and then another drummer. And then Zack.

He smiled at his father and then set down upon the platform the big bags that had made his shoulders strain the seams of his old brown suit. John hurried to help him. And Zack came to him and hugged him, his own father. John was so astonished he stiffened. He was being hugged in public, in town, in a country where it is understood that no man touches another man.

Far down near the Pullman car, the conductor called.

"All abooooord . . ."

They moved apart as if nothing had happened.

"Let me take one of those," John said.

Zack let him.

They stepped across the tracks. There loomed the Locomobile.

Zack said, "Great balls of fire. Whose is that, Pa?"

"She's yours, Zack."

"Mine? Great balls of fire!"

John tossed him the keys. The sun struck them.

*

The big car swept up past the new normal school, past the hospital and out of town. The silken muscles of a hundred horses smoothed and swelled under the hood. At last he'd given Zack something that pleased.

Great balls of fire.

In time to come, he meant to stand many times on that spot where he had tossed his son the keys, and maybe move back to a concrete bench for a new view of the very place. How right that a man can return and recapture.

Twenty miles out of town, when the great car had rushed through Black Canyon and the prairie fanned out ahead, they approached a spot marked by a monument. Lizzie and he had contributed.

Sealing the check into an envelope, Lizzie had remarked, "For our guilt."

Because the stone honored Sacajawea, the Indian woman who had been stolen as a child and who had guided Meriwether Lewis and George Clark back through the mountains. On this very spot, it was said, she recognized the land of her people and her lost home. Her *home,* which is where people were good to you and when you come back, they will be good again.

All through the canyon, where the deep walls isolated a man like falling dark, Zack had been silent. John waited patiently. Perhaps Zack listened to the quiet purr of the big car; more likely, he had been thinking of getting home, where all that was good waited. Once he did clear his throat, as if he were about to speak.

But John spoke first. "Pull over, Zack." Clean gravel was spread before the stone monument. "I've got to take a leak."

"Said and done," Zack said. Zack remained in the car while John got out, turned away, and relieved himself. How odd, he thought, that a man turns away, even when the only other around is his own son. The private parts, they called them. Private but to a man and his woman; his to her, hers to his. And to be concealed from others because of the Furies that union might loose.

He looked for a moment at the mountains, then turned, all buttoned up, and got back into the car. The door made a fine clunk.

"Pa, you looked so blamed serious. What were you thinking?"

He was about to lie, because that came easier. But he felt he owed the boy the truth, however it might sound to a young man.

"All right, Zack. The fact is, I've been thinking about time. And home." He took a breath and plunged. "And love." Ahead and far above a hawk hovered, high as his heart, a dark dot at the center of infinity.

"You think a lot like that, Pa?"

"I'm afraid so, Zack. Maybe I'd have—gone further if I hadn't." He fixed his eyes upon the hawk. "Or maybe if I had thought a lot more." When the hawk plummeted, he felt a chill like falling. He could hardly believe he'd blurted out about his having failed. But what a relief it was to reveal something private of himself—to relax, to relinquish; to hand over his failure to a younger and stronger man.

Now Zack would say, "It's all right, Pa. I'm here."

But Zack said nothing. So John had to ask, just to be sure that everything was still all right, "You ever think about that kind of thing?"

"Yes," Zack said, "I do."

And then he revealed to his father something of himself. He said, "That's why I've got to go."

Oh, Christ, he knew it when the hawk plummeted. Maybe they would and maybe they wouldn't, but they were sure as hell going to try to kill him. Should John beg openly? Plead his own need and Lizzie's fear and grief? But he knew, and it was like coming out of fever, that the time for that was past, and that there were areas in his son's life where he did not belong. Not now that they had spoken as men, and as friends.

A car is a child's toy.

Nevertheless, it was of the car that they spoke now, easily, joking, to bridge, as men will, the embarrassment of honest speech.

Zack dropped one hand outside the car to stroke the gleaming paint as he would the bright coat of a thoroughbred.

"She's a real peacheroo."

John laid his arm carelessly on the buttery leather behind Zack's shoulders. The cuff of his shirt slid jauntily from his coat sleeve. "And she'll be right here, raring to go." To his surprise he was able to say, then, what he had hoped never to say. "When you get back, Zack. When you get home again."

So they drove on, these confidants, this father and this son, while the Eumenides already gathered to visit upon them wrongs that had nothing at all to do with the World War.

Chapter
8

There were wise old ranchers all over the state who saw it coming. John Metlen was not one of them.

These old men had never heard of Beethoven or of Debussy's use of the whole-tone scale or of the Treaty of San Stefano, nor of the Categorical Imperative nor of Pragmatism: but they knew what worked out. They had remarked the early hibernation of the black bear, the badgers suddenly retiring to their holes, pulling the last warm days after them. They were concerned that summer of 1918 about the small snows of the previous winter and the dryness of that summer. Clouds loomed, piled up and seemed about to topple, but the rain was puny; the roots of the wild hay, the redtop, the timothy curled up like a bird's claw to receive the moisture, and then the sun came out. May, June, early July—the creeks ran thin, trickled, dried up. The trout, the redspecks, the rainbow and the cutthroats gasped in the murky hollows under the powdery banks.

The horse-drawn mowing machines lumbered into the scant hay. In the silence, ravenous grasshoppers worked away. In the hay camps, where the tents were pitched close by the expiring creeks, in the cool of the evening the hay hands hunkered down and softly spoke of mothers and whores and of buddies who had died. They ducked and entered their tents; they scratched a match on their trouser legs and lighted a Diehl lantern and their shadows leaped against the taut canvas. This terrible summer was no skin off theirs—a dollar a day is a dollar a day.

*

John's foreman was a man named Forbes, a Scot who'd been with John twenty years. John addressed him as Forbes and not as Angus; a man is proud of the name he was born with, and Forbes was proud.

"I sometimes think he knows more about the business than I do," John would say, not for a moment believing it but meaning his words as tribute to a hardworking man; it is doubtful that he noticed that no one ever disputed this. People looked on John as a man with too many irons in the fire and as far too generous. He was, in fact, a soft touch. No needy friend turned away empty-handed of a hundred or a thousand, and many who took from him felt obligated, which no man wants to feel. He was always puzzled by their withdrawal. Forbes never withdrew; but then, he never had intruded.

Therefore upon a summer evening Forbes stood first at the kitchen door and announced himself—"Forbes here"— and he wore a clean shirt and a necktie; it is more seemly that a man come to speak of a matter of moment should be clean and neat.

John and Lizzie sat opposite each other at an elaborate Victorian card table over yet another jigsaw puzzle meant to distract them from the heat and drought, though each hoped that the other looked on it as mere companionship. Through the open windows, beyond the lace curtains that stirred in the hot breeze, came the piping of killdeers gathered along what was left of Metlen Creek. Their song was as lovely as if the stream ran full.

One of the closets in the long dark hall held more than twenty of the hardwood puzzles, all of them—one every Christmas—gifts from Lizzie's father; no doubt he thought them a means of coping with the winters. The sameness of his gifts revealed him as a man who, like St. Mark, was not carried away by every blast of doctrine. Perhaps as he walked yet again into Brentano's he may have wished to break the pattern and send books instead, but as an old man he was afraid that if he altered choices, his daughter would think that he had altered, that his powers had failed. But to the last day of his life, Lizzie never thought his powers had failed.

Only this one, the last of them, still had all its pieces. On other boxes and in her clear Spencerian script, Lizzie had written, "3 pieces missing." Or "1 piece missing." John did not like these truncated puzzles. The piece he might be searching for might be the one missing. And what had become of the pieces? When they finished a puzzle they left it out for a few days as proof of their persistence, but they were scrupulous in putting it away. Yet for all their care, one puzzle after another dwindled, and in time, perhaps not in their time, someone would have to write, "All pieces missing."

This last puzzle, now that there would not be another, had an arcane significance. Unlike the others, the completed puzzle was not pictured on the cover of the box. It did not even have so much as a title. They were in the dark. Without even a title, they hardly knew where to begin.

"What do you suppose was in my father's mind," Lizzie said, "when he chose this one?"

"Some kind of test," John said.

"It's a test, all right."

They had a fair start on the perimeters of the puzzle,

choosing pieces with perceptibly straight edges, pushing them into little groups by color.

"Come right in, Forbes," John said. "Have a glass of iced tea."

Forbes seemed reluctant. Something unpleasant on his mind. Lizzie smiled, handed him his glass and left the room. She knew Forbes. He would no more have mentioned what he thought unpleasant before a woman than he would have cursed in her presence or picked at his teeth.

"Mr. Metlen?" Thus he recognized the difference between employer and employed; the easy traffic with first names has no place in business. "Mr. Metlen, two of the riders just rode in. They can't keep the cattle up there. They come down in the night."

John laid down a piece of the puzzle the color of pearl. "If we let them in the fields, Forbes," he said, "we'll have to start shoveling out hay first of November."

"You're right."

"And maybe it'll rain," John said.

Forbes said, "Maybe."

In John's head was a pretty clear image of dry roots crying for rain. Dry roots respond quickly. "There was a ring around the moon, and that means rain."

After quite a long while Forbes said, "Maybe."

"Well, a fellow's got to believe in something." Without belief a man was a ghost, a cipher. "Maybe a mild winter." Did Forbes guess that John hadn't money to buy hay? That, in fact, he was deep in debt?

"So let 'em into the fields, Forbes."

Forbes shoved his hand in his pants pocket and rattled change. He parted his lips to speak and paused, and then said, "Well then, goodnight, Mr. Metlen."

When Forbes had gone, John and Lizzie sat again at the little card table. Lizzie was methodical with the puzzles and quite strict about establishing the edges first; then fill in. John felt that her need to know the outline was a tacit criticism of his haphazard, easy choices. He liked to start on a color or texture—cloth, stone, flesh—and just see what came out of it. But it was this attention to the fragments and not the whole that had plunged him into this year's mess. And now suddenly the whole was all too clear.

"What did Forbes want?" Lizzie asked, looking up from a piece she had picked up.

"Oh—nothing much."

She started to speak and didn't, but his mind finished for her. Even if it does rain, it will be too late. A man's next breath is tentative. Everyone knows this, but John especially had made no moves that were proofs against ifs and maybes. And Forbes's last words struck him as portentous and as final. "Goodnight, Mr. Metlen" meant "Goodbye, Mr. Metlen"; and "Goodbye, Mr. Metlen" did not mean that Forbes was leaving, but that John Metlen was done for.

Now he had close to him each single pearl-colored piece, but when he had fitted them together and made a scallop shell, something was missing, still. Baffled, he searched the surface of the table for a final pearly piece. Was this puzzle that had never before been used already another puzzle with a piece missing? Could Lizzie's father for some reason have removed the whole from the box and lost a piece? But that man was a surgeon and had been trained to honor the meticulous. Then Lizzie surprised him. She said, "Ah-ha!" and proffered him a tiny rosy fragment. "Here's your foot," she said.

His foot?

"I see this is going to be Botticelli. *The Birth of Venus*. She comes to shore balancing on that shell." She was leading him, as she had always done, from whatever thoughts were proving so troublesome.

She said, "A funny thing about Venus. The idea of her makes many women doubtful of themselves and many men frustrated all their lives." He was astonished, as he had always been, at the number of things she knew.

"And yet," she said, "it was mere men and women who thought up this goddess."

*

The young recruits were ordered into local boards, handed little white cotton bags, made to shed their clothes and carry their valuables in the little cotton bags while the doctors had their way: probing into orifices, pulling back foreskins, looking for piles and for nits in the hair. Naked, the young men began to understand that there is little difference among men except for what they carried in the small white bags—a new pack of Fatimas or a square plug of tobacco, a ten-dollar bill or a few cents in change, a class ring, a grandfather's pocket watch or an Ingersoll turnip or no watch at all.

The poor-sighted and the flat of foot were sent home. The hale and hearty were handed papers for free passage on the railroad trains moving west to Camp Lewis in the state of Washington, and a good many older people who had paid good money were shunted off the main-lines in their Pullmans and sat waiting while hundreds of young healthy men shouted out the windows, passing west.

In Camp Lewis where the rainclouds hung low, they shed their clothes again; they were ordered to pack their civilian clothes into cardboard boxes, and the army sent those garments home as if they were already dead. Then Uncle Sam cut all their hair off.

Some of the young recruits had never seen a mother sit down at the kitchen table, clear away the sugar bowl and write a letter, except when somebody died. You didn't much expect a father to write. Fathers work hard and leave the writing to others. A mother knows letters are expected out there in the fog at Camp Lewis.

"My dear son," she begins.

That was true: he was dear. Oh, did that boy know what she and his father felt when they first saw he was all right and squalling like a healthy baby? Did he know what hopes they had for him? Most of all that his life would not be what theirs had been: not very much, when the cards were down.

"My dear son," she writes. "Your father like usual was up first this morning because like he says, he wants to be on top of things. That's your father for you."

She could not write, "Your father and I have lived together for so long we don't have many secrets from each other. This morning he didn't bother to pee against the side of the bowl so as not to splash."

Nor could she write, "Dear son, Sometimes I stand in the middle of this room and I wonder what happened and I think, Oh, dear God, I wish this room had more windows."

"My dear son, Your dad and I are both fine and hope you are the same. You always were a good boy . . ."

That was to remind him to stay that way at Camp Lewis, where there were bad women waiting.

*

Young ladies found writing to Camp Lewis hard, too. Their generation had grown up with the telephone and by means of it they sent notice of their arrivals and departures and told of their joy or sorrow at how things had turned out. The telephone had replaced the pen. In high school it had been a waste of time to untangle the snarl of thoughts that leaped at a young woman when she was required to record "My Most Interesting Experience," because what is interesting? And what, that will bear the light of day, is an experience?

The notes to Camp Lewis on tinted stationery or, alas, lined tablet paper were exhortations to Remember.

"Dear Owen, Remember that time out to the lake . . ."

Memory of that moon and the hiss of the prow of the canoe through the mirroring water might be proof against the temptations that were certain to abound around Camp Lewis. It was known that on the borders of the camp painted creatures, their heads piled high with curls, twisted their lips with smiles and waited; goodness and purity meant nothing to them. Not one of them so much as owned a hope chest nor had taken up a bit of dimity to sew for a little bundle of heaven. Sprinkled with rose toilet water, their fingers heavy with cheap rings, faces pale with talcum powder and scarlet with rouge, they offered a terrible experience almost bound to turn a decent boy's head, but one thing these creatures could not do was bake. They had no time for it. And so with the notes and memories went boxes of cookies moist to resist crumbling, packed firmly, and with love. It was thrilling to dwell on the arrival of that box and of how he would share it with his "buddies," as he called them.

And a striking amount of hair passed through the mails, some of it coiled neatly into lockets, sometimes a complete curl, snipped from where it didn't show too much and snugged in its own box. Unlike cookies, hair lasts; it neither wilts nor mildews. In the *Book of Facts* in the library on the corner of Rife and South streets, over by the table where the stereopticons are, it is written that in several important museums the hair of the great Napoleon rests under glass. In that hair, had we the proper instruments, we might detect—as arsenic is detected—traces of Wagram and of Waterloo. In *her* hair a young man would certainly detect traces of the love he himself had often and often mumbled into it. A lock of hair said what one hardly dared to write.

And the same with one of her own hankies sent to him, the corner embroidered with a vine-twisted rose or simple violet. Those were the days of roses and violets. Ah, and she would have been shocked but flattered at the use to which her young man had put that hanky. *That,* then, for those hussies who would have at him!

*

Zack Metlen, with no girl waiting for him, took the train east to Washington, D.C., where with a hundred others he studied codes on the top floor of a stone building. In the early fall, when the cottonwoods along Metlen Creek turned yellow and the frost lasted until noon, he was shipped off to France. John, who had never written a personal letter to anybody except Lizzie, did a pretty creditable job for a father.

> *Dear Zack,*
> *I often think of that day when I met you at the train when you came down from the university. I thought about that day when we drove out and we talked a bit and it suddenly came to me that we were a lot alike. And Zack, that made me happy.*

He had thought a long time about sending this, because it was pretty damn personal and any boy would have the right to say, reading it, "My father is a sentimental old fool." And Zack had never known how many nights his father had slipped quietly into his son's bedroom and watched the boy sleeping, adjusting his own breathing to his son's—why, until Zack was almost fourteen.

Because it is weak to confess fear.

He wrote nothing to Zack of his talk with Forbes, nothing of the drying streams and parched earth. Zack couldn't do anything about them. And having written that they were a lot alike, John could not write of the blind improvidence that threatened everything he owned, and worst of all Zack's future. Had John been a provident man, he could weather whatever came. However, he had not been a provident man.

But he wrote as a man without a worry.

> *We both love you. Pa.*

It might rain. But it did not rain. And if it had it would have been too late. But how a man does hope. Even when it's too late.

July had passed, and August, and September. The cattle had erased the short stubble in the hayfields; now they pressed close around the fenced haystacks. One wise old cow would rub and rub against a pole until a section of fence collapsed—one wise old cow in a hundred, her memory sharpened by hunger. Then a hired hand would ride in, drive the cattle out of the stackyard, repair the fence and ride a distance off, pull up his horse and wait—to discover which old cow was the troublemaker. When he spotted her he would pen her up. Maybe shoot her.

Now once again it was gorgeous October, a sapphire sky set in an Achaean frieze of aspen leaves. The mornings were crisp but the frost retreated along the cutting edge of the pale sun; the short warm afternoons were fragrant with the smoke from distant forest fires, and the haze hung like scrim over the mountains. Then it was a Sunday, the last of the month, and it was nine o'clock at night.

Every Sunday night John wound the tall clock in the hall; every night he stepped out of the house just before bed "to look at the stars"; the last thing every night he tapped the barometer, to prompt it to find its level. These things he did without fail and saw, in doing them faithfully, a search for immortality. Would not Death, Who itself had precise appointments to keep, think twice before meddling with a man's appointments so carefully kept? Only reluctantly did John accept any invitation for Sunday evening, knowing he'd have to make up an excuse to escape if it appeared he wouldn't be back by midnight.

"You told me yourself it's an eight-day clock." So Lizzie had spoken to him. "If you didn't wind it until Monday, the sky wouldn't fall."

"Wouldn't it? I wonder." He was only half joking. A long time ago he had committed himself, and a man who fails his commission has failed himself. Such a man might fail others.

So with satisfaction at doing the right thing, he wound the clock. In late October, 1917.

Then he stepped out to "look at the stars."

She smiled at the euphemism. "Why can't you use the word 'bathroom' like anybody else?"

She didn't understand that it's a privilege to be able to piss on your own land. If you can't piss on it, you don't own it. He couldn't piss on the lawn of the house in town they'd built when Zack started school. He looked on that town land, on that house, as not entirely his. Neighbors, with their herdlike propriety and standing just back from their windows where the angle of the light prevented them from being seen but not from seeing, forbade a man's pissing; their eyes cast a lien on his property.

He sighed when he'd finished, considering how similar a pleasure relieving himself was to satisfying hunger. Often, while pissing, he'd seen a star fall, plunge like a nighthawk on prey, and fade into infinity when it had spent itself. Gone, gone, gone. One fell now, through the nimbus of another of those rings around the moon.

He walked the path through the ryegrass back to the house.

He did not at once turn to the barometer, for Lizzie had come downstairs in a nightgown and a pretty silk kimono he had once bought for her in San Francisco. She was a tiny woman. Then he saw she was troubled.

"John, you stayed out so long I got worried."

"Why on earth worried?"

"I don't know," she said. "Let's have a cup of tea." And in a moment, "I can't put my finger on it."

The fire in the kitchen stove was long dead and the firebox so big it took forever to get it going. But she had a pretty little copper teakettle that nested in a stand above a spirit lamp. She got it down from the corner cupboard and set it up on the dining-room table. He liked to watch her use it; her long tapered fingers, so like Zack's, poured alcohol from a little bottle into the copper reservoir, scratched a match against the underside face of the sandstone fireplace, carried it lit to the table and awakened the pale blue flame. A funny, satisfying little ceremony, and hers alone.

He knew that her concern had nothing to do with his staying outside so long, and he waited for her to speak.

She said, "I was looking out the upstairs window, and I saw that circle around the moon again."

"Yes, I noticed."

"John, we've lived here twenty-five years, and we've never seen anything like so many of those circles."

He laughed. "Well, they don't seem to mean much. There's not a cloud. Not a breath of wind. The stars are bright as your rings."

And the same color, he thought. Green.

"Isn't it strange," she said.

"What is?"

"That I should have felt so—strange."

"Is it Zack?"

"Maybe. No. Maybe partly."

"Well," he said. Just "well," like one dismissing nonsense and about to make everything all right. "We can at least put a finger on the weather." And he walked then to the barometer on the wall, grateful that this small regular appointment had, at the moment, the power to distract her.

It is appropriate to mount a barometer beside the front door, so a man can open the door at once and verify what the barometer has told him, much as a man will turn to see with his own eyes what a rearview mirror has already told him; a man cannot trust instruments; their veracity is at best secondhand. John's was an aneroid barometer. The movement of its pointer depended upon the swelling and collapsing of a tiny, pleated, hollow metallic drum as the atmospheric pressure changed. It was not so accurate as a mercurial barometer but more handsome—and what were a few inches of pressure in any event. This aneroid was encased in heavy mahogany, trimmed with brass. The round glass was beveled. Because there were springs and levers and bearings in the linkage between the drum and the pointer, the pointer did not respond at once to the motion of the drum. But a gentle tap on the face of the instrument fixed that.

The pointer was poised straight up at twelve o'clock, so to speak, and meant Unchanged. The pointer seldom moved beyond eleven on the one side and one on the other.

He tapped the glass face and was struck dumb; the pointer trembled and then plunged headlong to the left to a place it had never pointed to before.

He had hoped to see hope; outside there had been stars,

and the world knows that instruments, which themselves depend upon man's fallibility, are fallible.

But when he spoke, his voice broke like a boy's whose voice is changing.

"It's broken," he said, but knew he was lying.

For instruments have no compassion; they tell the truth as they see it, and tell it at once. And however scrupulous John Metlen, he with his head in the clouds, had been in his foolish little efforts to keep the Eumenides at bay, the sky fell just the same. Within three hours the first of the horrible storms broke over the mountains to the west.

Those who had money had expensive hay shipped in from five hundred miles away. Those who had hay quickly saw that it was worth more than their cattle, more than their sheep; they sold their stock for a pittance and what they couldn't sell they shot. Those who could borrow borrowed. Those who could not went under. John Metlen lost the ranch and the sandstone house. Signed them away. His poor cattle stumbled into snowdrifts and died and froze. Snow covered them and their bodies heaved up under the crust like waves after waves, acres and acres of dead stock under the wind-blown snow. All winter the wind howled.

Later, when he was reminded of that winter by a board creaking as boards had creaked before the blast of the storm, by a draft whistling under a door as the land whistled under the wind, there sat in his mind a single image that was that winter—three wild horses.

Three wild horses, the last of two dozen that had roamed the foothills, they were descendants—colts of colts of colts of colts—of the mares and stallions the Spanish had brought with them in the nineteenth century; beautiful, strong, cat-like animals bought or stolen from the Moors, who bought or stole them from the Arabs; their blood was older than Plymouth or Jamestown. When the Spanish departed without gold and having murdered the Indians from whom they had hoped for gold, they turned the colts and yearlings loose, as useless. The colts died. The yearlings learned how to survive and grew, chose and defended mares and bred, and suddenly it was 1917. They had never known a halter, never felt a rope choking them to their knees. No man got closer to them than a mile, but John had often watched them with his field glasses, and it seemed to him that even as he trained the glasses on them, they froze, so instinctive was their distrust. They raised their smallish heads and froze, the mares, the yearlings, the magnificent stallion.

That spring, winter was still upon them. Only a few days before John had signed the ranch away, making such insecure arrangements as he could to save the house in town and the failing hotel. He was riding through the back pasture one late afternoon, having just counted another hundred cattle dead. He was cold, cold and finished. And so he must write Zack. He came in through the big back doors of the barn, unsaddled his horse and leaned against the stall. His legs felt useless.

He walked through the long dark barn to the front doors, and out.

There, standing close to the fence that protected a little hay saved for the milk cows and the saddle horses, were the three wild horses. A mare, a yearling, and the chestnut stallion. Their ribs were gullied, their eyes dull and sunken. Hunger had driven them down from the hills; hunger had tamed them as no man could. Seeing him, they hardly moved; death sniffed at their poor heels.

The mare was pregnant and about to drop the foal. She had conceived last summer when the purple lupine flowered in the secret parks in the deep timber, when the stars at night had quite a different configuration; she had conceived according to Nature's will that the breed continue, but at the very moment when the stud mounted her and his heart missed a beat and his eyes glazed at the moment of ejaculation, something Else, something malignant that scorned the promise of the spreading lupine, marked that colt for death in that mare's womb.

He walked past, through the snow into the house.

"I'm home, Lizzie," he called.

She no longer asked where he'd been, what he'd been doing. Now, for the life of him, he could not speak to her of the three horses out there, nor could he tell why these, of all the starving animals, made him the sickest. Why in the name of God had they come to him when there were a half-dozen ranches easier for them to reach? Why, in the name of God?

Already it was getting dark. Before long he wouldn't see the horses even if he looked out. He need not even think of them when, even if he looked out, he couldn't see them.

"Let's have some coffee, Lizzie." Lord, the pots she'd brewed at odd hours this past winter. In a strange way their little times together meant even more than before, and that was always much. Tiny, tiny things had gotten so important. At two o'clock one morning he'd got up, gone downstairs in the cold dark, found a plane and fixed a door that hadn't shut for twenty years. Were the little things big now because the big things were slipping?

No, he would not look out at the horses. Even if he did, he probably couldn't see them through the snow that was spitting again. But he did look, because he had to see that he could not see them. Maybe they'd stumbled off to another place where another man, a more careful man, had more hay left. That man, then, must make the decision.

He looked out. The three ghostly shapes, the mare, the yearling, and the stallion, had all but dissolved into the consuming twilight. They had moved a few feet from the fence, away from the hay behind the stout poles; a ton of it at least, a ton of good redtop and timothy and clover. They had moved to a spot cleared by the hooves of many other horses. He watched and saw them lift their legs, and then he saw what they were doing. They were pawing. They were pawing up pebbles from under the hard crust, and they lowered their heads and ate the pebbles, driven by the primal urge to fill the stomach, if but with stone.

"Lizzie, I'm going out."

As he approached the three, they froze. The yearling

and the mare raised their heads. The stallion was too weak to rear between them and the man. But, wild-eyed, he tossed back his head and snorted, out of the need to be what he had been.

So John opened the gate into the hay pen.

Somebody wanted the Jersey milk cows; they'd be fed. Someone would want the saddle horses; they were good ones with Morgan blood. Nobody wanted three unbroken and defeated nags. They were useless except maybe in some scheme quite beyond his understanding. But now the mare's colt would be born. And opening the gate, he knew it was time to write to Zack and say, We're finished.

But Fate hadn't finished with the Metlens. Not by a long shot.

Chapter 9

John Metlen was among hundreds of ranchers in the mountain states to lose his holdings. In some parts of that country, the winter had been even worse and had started earlier. Many of the ruined ones had been as improvident as John and suffered for the same reasons—a cavalier attitude toward money; maybe they felt they were of so fine a clay they didn't need money, or that money was their birthright and they had a right to spend it. They had been contemptuous of other men who, as children, respected their piggy banks and fed them regularly.

But the reckoning comes. Let us say, a costly illness. Doctors and hospitals know that some people will hand over their last dime to keep somebody alive.

There may come a fire, or a flood—and they, the foolish ranchers, were suddenly bereft and penniless, as helpless in adversity as their oldest cowboy, who had counted on them to provide a room and a bed to die in. They could hold their heads no higher than the chore boy who hauled off the stinking manure from the barn or the man who milked the cows.

The West had so short a history that a man could not, suddenly impoverished, turn to pride in birth and family; could not wrap about himself the robe of his ancestors. It was only the Indians who could do that, and point to the ancient graves. The rancher was *sui generis* and by himself had come from rags to riches; once he had lost his place in local society, he would no longer be greeted with deference at poker tables and in the lobbies of great hotels, nor would his wife be asked to pour at teas. Such aristocracy as existed in the West was based squarely on ownership of land; without land, a man had only the clothes he wore and his own two hands.

Some who were ruined went as wards to brothers or sisters; some vanished to California. The luckiest were kept on as foremen on what had been their own land; banished from the big house and sent to the bunkhouse, they lived in a strained relationship with the new owners. Some began to drink.

*

Aware of the severity of the winter, the late spring, the scarcity of hay and the starving cattle, a Chicago broker had made inquiries of banks in the region that held paper on likely ranch property. He liked fishing; he tied his own flies, but admitted that the Royal Coachman you bought in the hardware store was as attractive as what he could manage with feather and silk. He took good care of his Shakespeare reel and kept it disassembled in a chamois pouch. He liked hunting and had spent weeks in the Michigan wilderness, wanting no fancy vittles and no air mattress, thank you, under his sleeping bag. But those places in the Michigan wilderness were rented. A man wants his own place. He wanted to be a landed gentleman.

His wife, who had Swift connections, was not hard to convince; among her pleasantest memories were weeks spent in Yellowstone Park, where she made easy friendships with the rangers and the young ladies who worked as waitresses in the Old Faithful Inn, getting together sums for the next year's tuition at state universities; she thought some of them exceedingly well-spoken. She loved horseback riding, the sharp scent of pine, the aroma of frying bacon and the first rays of the rising sun that fell on the Grand Tetons. She had dreaded the round of parties she must return to.

The Metlen ranch fell into their hands.

John Metlen was not asked to stay on as manager. He would have refused, had he been asked; and he was happy that Forbes was able to stay on and to run things after the place had been restocked and the carcasses dragged away and burned. The Chicago people were glad of the big sandstone house; they had many friends who liked horseback riding and picnics in clearings in the timber, and they had two active children. So all was well with them; they appreciated the unexpectedly quite nice furnishings in the big, cool house, and the china and silver were above reproach—and out there in the wilderness, mind you. They were glad to have been of help to the poor souls who were leaving.

"It might have been us," said the broker, touched for a moment with compassion. He gazed across his new acres to Black Canyon.

"I hardly think so," his wife had said, smiling. She did understand his intention to mildly frighten himself. We do like to scare ourselves, like children, when we know everything is going to turn out all right. "And I thought the Metlens quite well-spoken."

*

The "poor souls" who were cast off were lucky to have the house in town. John had the gumption not to mortgage it. They drove in from the ranch for the last time just before supper. People were already off the streets. They went to bed early and lay awake in the long summer twilight. They hoped nobody would knock on the door. Nobody did. There was surely pity afoot, the last thing in the world a man wants. There is no defense against pity. A man can only lift his chin, and stare straight ahead. He knows he is granted pity because he's not worth anything else.

Of course, John felt himself an outcast. He shut the big Locomobile away in the carriage house where no man might see it and be reminded of John's folly. Besides, the car was Zack's. He had bought it for Zack—a bribe to keep Zack on the ranch. And now the ranch was gone.

He had written Zack of the foreclosure. "I'm afraid we're done." But they had had no reply. Maybe the letter was under the ocean. What they had heard from Zack in the spring of 1918 was a cheerful report about a "fellow in my outfit." This fellow was Zack's age and was, apparently like Zack, with "principles." He had left the Massachusetts Institute of Technology to join the Signal Corps.

"We've got some pretty nifty ideas," Zack wrote. Were these ideas the "principles" they held in common? John would have liked to sit down with that young fellow's father and inquire what he thought about "principles" and to what lengths he had gone to keep his own son safe at home. Why would a young man, even for "principles," leave a college, one of the best in the world, and go to France?

Then it began to dawn on John that both this young man named Kaufman and Zack might look on the Signal Corps as a means to some end. In the Signal Corps they meant to find something, some experience, that the Massachusetts place didn't offer, nor the science department at the state university. Had Zack not been entirely honest about his reason for joining up? There is an awful lot of hiding behind "principles."

John was now not an easy man to live with. He slept late; he complained of aches and pains and looked on them as a warning of his end. He refused invitations. And Lizzie—

Lizzie went about her days much as before, as if nothing at all had happened.

But John was a man, as his father had said, with his head in the clouds. He sat at the table in the kitchen in his bathrobe, a garment he never used to wear, and Lizzie asked him what he'd like for lunch. He guessed some tomato soup and a few crackers. It was probably all he deserved.

"Damn it, I can't understand what happened."

She turned from the cupboard, sat down opposite him and rested her chin on the palms of her hand.

"Well, what has happened—really?"

Here she sat in a house that was barely more than adequate, that had been meant only as a perching place so that Zack wouldn't have to board out, and she could ask what happened. John was what had happened—really.

He had no intention of saying what he said next. "I tried to mortgage the hotel. Connard laughed. Did you know there's a new hotel going up? On the right side of the tracks? I didn't know there was a wrong side of the tracks."

"Well?"

"That nice young manager we had last couldn't afford to stay. Lizzie, it's padlocked. Packrats will be in there next."

"Well?"

She put her garden-brown fists across the table and knotted his with hers. He saw the shameful white stripe where the emerald used to be.

She said, "Do you believe I love you?"

Well, yes, he did.

"Then believe I didn't marry you because you were avaricious."

Why, she was laughing at him. And then suddenly she wasn't.

"John," this extraordinary woman said. "I married you because you are a poet."

They were still holding hands across the table when the courthouse clock struck noon.

*

If the town had a focal point, it was the bell of the court-house clock. When the clock struck, wave after wave of sound flowed out and settled down and gilded the hour; and some-body, somewhere, paused to set his pocket watch. John had often seen the eyes of a man to whom he was talking go vacant as the clock struck, as if the man were remembering a pressing appointment. Ever since the clock with four faces had been hauled up by block and tackle twenty-seven years before, it had been the arbiter of time in Grayling, but no one knew for sure if or when its hands were corrected by infor-mation on the telegraph at the Union Pacific depot; if it was corrected, who did it? Must have been the responsibility of somebody in the courthouse; but it was strange that whoever did it didn't mention it. After all, a boy in school reports that he's been allowed to clap all the erasers together and to open and close the tall windows with the window stick. A person likes to be known as the one chosen, boy and man. Was it Skinny Nelson, the chief of police? Probably not, for Nelson must always be ready to enforce the law; when he was to correct the clock, he might be called on to investigate a scream or to net a mad dog. The superintendent of schools was a better bet. She was a dignified lady with a pince-nez on a long black cord, and in charge of all who taught that time was a commodity whose proper use led to success, a good reputation and a bank account. Maybe it was she who set her watch by the telegraph, and then hurried, as a big proud woman hurried, back to the courthouse and called up the right time to somebody able to scramble up the iron ladder and set each of the four faces.

Or nobody set it. Maybe it was always wrong, and the world had not yet so changed that ten minutes one way or the other made much difference. That was a comfortable thought. Maybe too much is made of time. What is it anyway, but moving shadows? Moving shadows, long moving shad-ows now in late October, inching toward All Soul's and the Carnival of Death.

John remembered Mexicans and such a carnival, the

sound of flutes and whistles like little cries, and cakes shaped like human skulls and jumping-jack skeletons that clattered like dry bones. He thought he understood the merriment—who has not whistled in the dark? But he seldom thought of death. How strange now, as the train waited and the locomotive hissed and shuddered, to see a coffin removed from the baggage car.

It was a plain pine box, and the colored man did not pull it away from the baggage car until a woman had stepped down from the chair car behind the baggage car. When she had touched the ground, she turned back, and from above somebody handed her down a little child of no more than a year.

It was clear enough that the dead one was the husband, the father, and that this woman came from one of the Scandinavian families outside of town.

She began the walk to the baggage car, the little child's head against her shoulder. She walked slowly, as if the neat graveled path beside the tracks were treacherous, but as she approached John saw that the trouble was her cheap, new, unforgiving shoes. The sun splintered on the hard patent leather. Her thick hair was like ripened wheat, braided and coiled about her head; surely more than one person had remarked, "Oh, you have lovely hair!" and she had gone to bed wrapped in the compliment. But above the handsome braids, she had put on a hat.

It was a cheap hard hat, a small black saucer from which depended two shiny red plaster cherries, a hat that said, I am the hat of a woman who suddenly needed a hat. The hat was unaccustomed to her head; it sat warily above the wheat-colored coils.

She no longer wept. Like many another riding on a train, she had realized as the telegraph poles flashed by against the empty horizon that tears are useless. When she and the baby reached the baggage cart, she touched the coffin.

As the train pulled away, the dozen watchers at the station drifted off; the presence of a coffin is sobering. Nobody wants to be involved. Everybody will be involved soon enough.

Only John remained.

No one else had yet appeared. Had she telephoned someone? Had she telegraphed? Few of the farmers outside town had telephones, and this young woman might be dismayed at the complication of sending a telegram. A letter asking for help would have arrived no sooner than the train that brought the body.

After a few moments, the colored man dropped the heavy tongue of the cart, and looked at the young woman for instruction. Her concern was far beyond the next five minutes, and the next five hours. The next five minutes would solve themselves. But the next five years? Because then the little child would ask a question.

"What's a father?"

She must say, "A father is the one who comes home at night. A father is the man who gives a woman a little child."

Her words might do for a year or two—explain who the man was and why the child was. But when the boy was eight or nine, he'd begin to guess that every man has a story, and without that story's being told, the father is a cipher. So one day, in the evening when it's quiet and easier to speak because the dusk hides the concern and the hesitation in another's eyes, the boy would ask, "What was he like? Tell about my father."

And she would tell a story. And no matter what the man was like, she would tell it in a certain way because she could not—she could not—bear to tell it in any other way.

But now she stood dumb, glancing first at the two cheap suitcases beside the track, and then at the colored man.

John stepped forward. "Please? I'm John Metlen."

"Christina Andersen," the young woman said.

The Scandinavians in that country all spoke more than a little English. John turned to the colored man, whose name was Brown. "Brown, if you'd be so kind and stay with Mrs. Andersen, I'll hop across the street and rout out Thorpe."

Thorpe was the new undertaker. John had heard of no recent death in town; Thorpe must be free.

"Glad to," Brown said.

"Mrs. Andersen," John said, "have you some papers in your pocketbook?"

She understood. "Please take them."

"Thorpe is a good man," John said. "Mrs. Thorpe was a schoolteacher." He understood the Scandinavian respect for learning. It was not to be imagined that Mrs. Thorpe had married a careless man.

Christina Andersen said, "Terrible things happen."

"I'm afraid that's true," John said. He could hear in the distance the water in the river running over the rocks.

Thorpe came with the hearse very shortly and took away the pine box. "Was someone to meet you, Mrs. Andersen?" John said, and was concerned that his meaning might not be clear. "Is anyone coming—to take you to your house?"

"I don't know." And John imagined telephone calls and attempted telephone calls. Possibly someone relayed a message and possibly not. In fact, no one had come.

John said, "I'll get my car. I'll come back for you and the baby and your bags. Do you mind waiting, Mrs. Andersen?"

She said, "I will wait."

He returned in less than ten minutes. He had hoped that she would be gone, that friends had arrived whose familiarity with her and her husband and of their peculiar past would make them better consolers than he and Lizzie might be.

But she was there, holding the baby. He put the bags in the tonneau of the Locomobile, helped Mrs. Andersen and the baby into the front seat and took them to Lizzie.

Lizzie met them in the hall.

"Lizzie," John said softly, "This is Mrs. Christina Andersen."

Lizzie said, "Oh. Oh, yes."

John glanced at her. It was a curious salutation. It sounded almost as if Lizzie were expecting her.

And that, in a sense, was true. For with the appearance of

Mrs. Andersen, an important moment in Lizzie's past had become instantly clear, just as a name that has steadfastly eluded memory will leap forward—and for no other reason than that a small cloud has passed before the sun. What wakened Lizzie's understanding was the hat on the woman's head and the braids beneath it. Sun and wind had roughened the porcelain skin and slanted the first fine lines about the wide-set eyes, but it was she who had once stood rapt before the window of Huber's Jewelry.

A dozen years ago their eyes had met in what Lizzie had taken as a courtesy between strangers. But in a moment she had become quite uncertain of what that glance meant, and she'd been tempted to turn back and speak—but saying what? She had not turned back, and from time to time over the next years she would suddenly pause, thinking, wondering, uncomfortable with a sense of the incomplete and at a loss to understand its importance.

Now suddenly, she understood that glance. It was one familiar to almost everybody, a glance that simply confirmed a previous appointment. Somehow, that appointment was now at hand.

In the living room, Christina Andersen sat bold upright on the sofa, the baby asleep beside her. John brought in the cardboard suitcase and placed it on the sofa. Mrs. Andersen turned from the waist and opened it. On top were several neatly folded diapers. Beneath them, John noted, were a man's clothes, the color and material quite at odds with the patent-leather shoes and hat with cherries. The better clothes that complemented her outfit must now clothe the man in the pine box.

Mrs. Andersen moved to change the sleeping baby's diaper.

"Let me," Lizzie said. "I love babies. I don't want to forget how."

"You are good," Christina Andersen said, and in a moment the room was sharp with the odor of ammonia. Lizzie worked. Christina Andersen talked, "I am yet thirty-three years," she began.

Her husband was thirty-four. Although they had taken out first papers, they were not yet naturalized, so Waldemar, the husband, could not fight for his new country, but he knew the Pledge of Allegiance.

The baby woke, and whimpered. Lizzie picked him up, cradled him close, rocked him. And while Christina Andersen continued to talk, Lizzie's heart struck hard against her ribs. The baby's breath was hot and impure.

His mother talked as if speech had been dammed too long.

The brother of Waldemar, Anders Andersen, lived in Cedar Rapids, Iowa, sold ice and owned an automobile. He had sent pictures, and he had sent a check.

Waldemar, her husband, kept pigs on their farm out here. She hated pigs. The boars sometimes ate their young. She hated a pig's eyes. Of all the animals, only pigs can follow you with their eyes. They don't have to move their heads to see, like a horse or a cow.

Lizzie nodded, but didn't follow closely. Look now, how foolish she had been. The baby was exhausted, and no wonder, by the long trip and by his mother's grief. His small miraculous hand was motionless upon her breast; she bent over the warm, damp little head and he breathed evenly and slept again.

It was to a big pig show that Anders had invited them. They could have used the check for something better. She wanted a de Laval cream separator. But Anders promised picnics, rowing on a lake, music at night in a hall where Scandinavians danced polkas. They took the train, but the dancing never came to pass.

Instead, in his new clothes, he had gone to the pig show with Anders.

"That's all I have," she said. "Those clothes."

Waldemar and Anders walked in the pig building large as a field with windows in the roof. There was dust everywhere, for tractors had come in through the big doors and pulled out three dead pigs that had come to win prizes.

The brothers remained two hours in the pig building talking with friends of Anders's; then they left and went to a saloon, where they drank beer.

Standing at the bar, Waldemar suddenly said, "I feel funny."

"Two days, he was dead." Christina's eyes moved from Lizzie's to John's. Her eyes said that the death of the pigs and the death of Waldemar were not coincidental. The frightening fact about people even temporarily mad is that they sometimes seem to have gotten hold of the truth.

A Dr. J. S. Koen, of the Bureau of Animal Husbandry, detected a similarity between the dead and dying hogs and the influenza striking people in Cedar Rapids. He knew that to the west, in the cavalry post of Fort Riley, they had for months been burning nine thousand tons of germ-carrying horse dung, and the stench hung over the country in clouds.

After a windstorm that sent soldiers of the 97th Division on the post gasping to their tents, one of the cooks in the outfit took to his cot and died choking. Another hundred or so followed him underground. Shortly after the 97th Division landed in France, the poilus over there came down with the disease. Dr. Koen called it the swine flu. Twenty-one million died. One moment a man was well and happy. The next moment he wanted to lie down. His arms and legs ached. His mouth was inflamed, and his throat. He gasped. The air pockets in his lungs filled with mucus. He choked and he died.

*

On the porches of Grayling, Montana, the pumpkins on the top steps winked and glared; it was a time of bats and witches; on the corner of Rife and Pacific streets, the streetlight was faint through the tangle of bare branches. Children in masks and sheets hurried along the sidewalks, thrilled with intimations of mortality.

A hard freeze struck the town three days after Halloween. The milk in the bottles left on the back porch froze and expanded and burst through the cardboard caps; the freeze burst the radiators of Dodges, Buicks and Maxwells left un-drained, a pretty good argument for the air-cooled Franklin if you had the extra cash. A fortune was in store for the man who would invent a liquid that wouldn't freeze like water, that wouldn't boil dry like alcohol or gum up the water pump or rot the hoses like kerosene. In winter, as it was, you had to drain your radiator every night or step outside around midnight, start your car, and then cover the radia-tor with a blanket.

The pumpkins froze, too. When the temperature rose on the last days of Indian summer, the pumpkins collapsed, their carved mouths drawn in and slack like those of old, toothless men.

It had seemed to Lizzie that Zack was close when she carved the pumpkin and set it out. It was for him she carved it. What harm could come to a boy whose mother has set out a pumpkin with love? She thought it glorious to have been granted the gift to delight in the odor of a candle toasting the flesh of the pumpkin's cover, and then to savor the memory of every other one. Not many were as lucky as she to wake each morning loving life, eager for a first word with John, for the first sip of coffee.

"I'm glad I saved the seeds," she said of that last pump-kin. Whether to plant them or to toast them, John didn't know, because she finished, "John, I think I'll just go up and lie down."

John sat dumb beside her hospital bed. It was she herself who had said, Nothing matters but each other.

For two days and nights she was lucid, and spoke of long-ago things, evoking the past to erase the present. She spoke of a pack trip to a lake, and of a time when the loons called all night long.

"I remember, Lizzie."

Memory was life in itself.

She was lucky she was still conscious three days after the Armistice; he had brought the newspaper to her. Maybe she died happy.

Never once did she speak of love. Their love spoke for itself.

Her coffin and Martin Connard's were among the last of the fine coffins now available. Thorpe the undertaker said he was about to throw up his hands—you couldn't get good coffins for love or money.

Chapter
10

So early in 1919, Harry Connard stepped into his father's shoes, and although old Martin Connard's shoes were impressive, Harry wore them with élan. Before the old man's death, Harry had several times slipped into those shoes, and had bought several thousand acres of worthless sagebrush, rocks and dry ravines, because a geologist was convinced that oil flowed somewhere beneath the surface. Since the land had been looked over some years before for possibilities and found lacking, it was thought that Harry had overstepped himself even in those shoes. There were some who would not be disappointed to see Harry come a cropper.

A man of five foot ten likes to think of himself as above average height, and indeed there are millions upon whom he can look down. The man of six feet has things pretty well in control and looks down on or at eye level with almost every other man in the room. But Harry stood six foot two; his head was above other heads in dining rooms and ballrooms from Chicago to San Francisco. He waist was slim as a boy's; he was suspected of practicing calisthenics in his bedroom in the big brick house in Grayling, or in the huge log house on the ranch where the floors were of hardwood and covered with Navajo rugs and the walls with the prepared heads of wild animals he had shot here and there.

He carried himself with the easy arrogance of a man who has gone to a good private school and to a university where nearby Lake Washington and Puget Sound were perfect for sailing. His friends out there were the sons and daughters of shipping and lumber, and they continued to drive to Grayling in their motorcars or in compartments on the train, and enjoyed the life on the ranch, the camping trips, the fishing, the local rodeos. Harry Connard did not ride in rodeos—rodeo riders are from quite a different class. His hired hands performed well at Frontier Days in Grayling and in Butte and across the divide in Salmon, Idaho, where everybody had fun. But Harry sat a horse handsomely, and often trailed cattle from the ranch to the railroad.

"Funny thing he hasn't married" was sometimes heard.

Chuckles. "That Harry don't have to marry." And those who so spoke were somewhat right. Long past were the willing girls from the wrong part of town and the young ladies picked up in hotel lobbies; the sisters of his university friends thought him a good catch, and so did a young woman from Butte who had quite as much money as he did.

Young ladies in chiffon frocks with beaded bandeaux about their pretty marcelled heads danced with him at the St. Francis, the Olympic, and the Thornton Hotel in Butte. They rode the dark piny trails with him into the mountains, suffering stiffness in their thighs and pain in their pretty rumps, and Harry Connard went to bed with them there in blankets scented by fresh bear grass, covered over with a tarp that smelled of sun and rain, and he was the first up, and turned and relieved himself, and the naked young woman knew despair.

No wonder her brother, whose copper mine riddled that largest hill in Butte, announced that he would skin Harry Connard alive. But after all, the young woman herself said that Harry had not forced her. Why should he?

"When the right time comes, Harry will settle down. He's bound to."

And yet this enviable man was cankered with self-doubt, just like the rest of us, and for what would seem to us an odd reason. Men are supposed to hold their liquor well, and as far as the world knew, Harry Connard did. He himself knew better. He was not a thoughtful man, but he came to wonder if there was any correlation between the buffeting restlessness he sometimes felt, that drove him beyond the safe borders of his own county, and the blank hours, the time lost between one footfall and another, between the raising of a glass and the putting it down, the hours never recovered and forgotten only slowly and with a hot embarrassment. He had never been questioned about these lacunae; therefore he had done nothing violent or dangerous. But there were places to which he never returned because he was afraid that there he had lost control, acted up: played the fool. If he had, you might just as well emasculate him. So Butte was still all right, but Helena was not, nor Miles City, nor Fargo.

In Grayling, Harry Connard was very, very careful.

Those who drove by the square brick Connard mansion in Grayling where, on either side of the wide stone steps, scarlet geraniums thrived in stone urns; those who saw Harry Connard stride down those broad steps, dressed in a three-piece suit and wearing a big-brimmed cowboy hat of 3X nutria, knew that he was a catch and that the girl who caught him would be fortunate: the woman he married would instantly become a queen.

Therefore you might well ask, "But why on earth, with the

entire world within his reach, did Harry Connard propose to a nineteen-year-old girl in a town called Salmon, Idaho?"

What could be in Salmon, Idaho? Who could be there? Gold and silver were in Salmon's past, but not much; the metals petered out before anybody local had amassed enough to build a great house with a cupola and an iron stag on the lawn. Most of the gold drained off to the East into the hands of men shrewder than the prospectors who found it. Prospectors are dreamers hankering for God knows what—maybe a piece of land—but they like to set up drinks. They still tell of one such man who tossed gold nuggets on the barroom floor and watched people scrabble on their hands and knees.

Salmon was a town of fifteen hundred; small houses, some of frame, some of local brick, dotted both sides of the Salmon River, connected by a high, rusting iron bridge that trembled. Once on the other side, the sensitive, safely over the wild water below, felt proud to have cheated death a little, and even considered what a precious gift life is. Ranchers drove into town for groceries, saddles, harness, Sloan's liniment at the Red Cross Pharmacy. Half a dozen bars were open for drinking and gambling.

In three restaurants a man might order steak and, in the wintertime, oysters brought in by a poky little railroad train that crept in twice a week. A treasure recently recognized was the gorgeous scenery. Salmon was located near the Primitive Area; the vast forest lands were hugged around with lofty sawtoothed mountains. Footloose Easterners, tired of the Laurentians and even of the Alps, found these virgin peaks remote and charming; a trip down the clear, treacherous river, running awesome rapids on a wooden raft, was an experience few friends back East could match, and a good story to tell at the Campfire Club.

When the war ended, a handful of working ranches down on their luck had already taken in a handful of Eastern dudes, so called because of their neat clothes, their tailor-made cigarettes and their ignorance of Western-style saddles. These misplaced strangers, anxious to get in touch with the primitive for the sake of their souls, hauled themselves out of bed at six in the morning, washed in cold water and appeared at the long breakfast table for flapjacks, fried eggs and fried ham. They were proud when a rawboned cowhand spoke kindly, and they followed him on horseback up and down frightfully steep and narrow trails. When darkness came, they sat around the fire.

On Saturday nights they "went into town" with the cowboys and stood at the bar, learned to roll their own cigarettes and toss off straight whiskey—even the women among them who never before in their lives had stood at a bar, nor moved over to make way for a stranger.

In Salmon they went on shopping sprees for John B. Stetson hats, for Justin boots and Levi Strauss overalls. McCloud's—the Big Store—imported buckskin gloves from the southern part of the state where the Indians were exiled, gloves with long, intricately beaded gauntlets in floral designs, beaded moccasins, ladies' purses, the labor of patient squaws who sat huddled against the howling wind in smoke-filled wickiups. Many went blind. They couldn't afford glasses.

It was in McCloud's—the Big Store (little wire baskets ran overhead carrying money to and fro)—that Harry Connard first set eyes on Anne Chapman. He had gone there to set eyes on her.

She was, of course, only a woman. Many men and many women had already said that, and it did not in the least make the women feel better that they had said it.

The experience of a couple of dudes summed it all up for them. This couple of dudes, a man and wife, went into the Big Store shortly after having arrived in Salmon. They bought a costly Shakespeare collapsible fishing rod, a reel, a creel, and a dozen Silver Doctor dry flies. Fishing with dry flies is considered more sporting than fishing with live bait; it is a pleasure to deceive a fish with bait made of silk and feathers.

Overhead the little wire baskets moved. They thanked the young man who had praised the Salmon River as alive with fish, and they went through an arch into the dry-goods department. Some moments later they returned to the sunny street and got into their big blue Marmon touring car.

For a moment the husband sat without putting his hands on the wheel.

His wife asked, "Do you have your keys?"

"My keys?"

"To the car. The keys. You haven't looked in your pocket. Look in your pockets."

"Yes. My pockets."

"I think you're bemused."

He looked at her, as if attempting to locate her voice.

She continued, "When that young woman spoke to you, you looked at your feet, like a schoolboy. Was she so dazzling, then? Were you so blinded?"

He shook his head, as if testing it.

She continued. "It isn't difficult to appear attractive when you're eighteen or twenty years old. No great thing. Oh, Nature has seen to it that a young woman appears attractive."

Then he spoke. "I never in my whole life," he said. The old men on the walls of Troy had never in their whole lives either. As for the wife, she touched her hair below her hat to see if it had escaped its net. She had never in her life, either, but strangely she felt no jealousy, not even envy, only a sadness.

Harry Connard had caught the scent of someone extraordinary in Salmon. He had heard tell. Drummers stopping in to cash checks. Cattle buyers. Mining men come into Salmon to look over properties that might once again be valuable, thanks to new machinery and new methods. What Harry Connard heard was tantalizing, because although it lacked substance, everything was repeated by yet another. What he heard was that at a certain hour a young woman walked from the edge of town where she lived with her grandfather, and down the long street, and passed inside the Big Store near the approach to the bridge. No more than that. But it was clear that in Salmon people watched when she walked.

About this one who walked, he'd heard no scandal. No trysts mentioned. No conquests. Conquests not even suggested. Her name alone was known—that was about the extent of anybody's intimacy, and Harry Connard would bet that her name was known only because somebody other than she had been asked what her name was. "My name is Anne Chapman" was a statement probably few had heard. Anne was a beautiful name. It had magic. Did she?

Suppose he said to her not "What is your name?" but rather "My name is Harry Connard." Just as her name had drifted east across the Continental Divide, so certainly word of him had drifted west. She was, after all, a young woman. He was, after all, Harry Connard. He, too, was watched when he walked the street.

"That's Harry Connard. I'd like to be in his shoes."

A grandfather kept creeping into this new myth. Was that because he had married an Indian woman or because the girl's parents had vanished? If the grandfather was in some way formidable, Harry Connard could handle that. He certainly could handle the fact that the girl was a quarter Indian. The fact rather appealed to him. He liked the Pocahontas story. The story didn't end quite right. Pocahontas should have married Captain John Smith instead of that man named Rolfe, but she and Rolfe went to England and moved in London's best circles.

What grandfather would not be pleased to have a granddaughter walk out into the town on the arm of a Connard? Maybe the grandfather was part of the myth to make clear the girl's laudable responsibility for an old man. Responsibility in a woman is a good thing, too.

So in the late summer of 1919 Harry Connard drove over the Continental Divide—the Hill, they called it—to Salmon. Heavy rains had left the road at the bottom on the Montana side a sticky morass. The clay, as if living, oozed and glued itself into the indentations of the tire treads, smoothed the wheels and robbed them of traction.

On the far side of a bad mudhole he had managed to cross by rushing at it, Harry Connard stopped the black Peerless touring car, pulled on a pair of coveralls over his suit, got out the heavy Weed chains, stretched them flat before the rear wheels, rolled the car up on them and fastened them around the wood-spoked wheels. You'd think the Weed people could have managed a better fastener, one that didn't pinch the fingers and raise blood blisters.

And what a relief to have reached the top of the hill. Going down, he'd at least have gravity on his side. It was cool up there; the last of a recent rain had turned to snow. He unwrapped a ham sandwich and wondered what on earth he was doing in pursuing a will-o'-the-wisp. Already he had driven fifty-five miles. The town of Salmon lay far down the valley.

In Salmon, he pulled up before a small red-brick hotel, a refuge for drummers, and a shabby one. He liked a good hotel, and because he did and others did, he had invested a comfortable amount in the new one going up across the tracks from the old Metlen Hotel—the right side of the tracks.

He felt he needed a drink.

It was now four in the afternoon, according to one of the newfangled wristwatches the soldiers had been wearing in France. His room was across the street and four blocks up from the Big Store, and he could see anyone who left there at five when the place closed. Looking down into the street from the second floor of the Shenon House, he was privileged, without knowing that he was privileged, to look on a scene that, except for the moving pictures, would never again be duplicated—he was looking into a street where the number of motorcars almost exactly equaled the number of horses.

He considered staying right where he was—he might even draw up a chair to the window to watch. He wondered if those who rode horses, who sat in buggies, in spring wagons, who sat at the wheels of Model T Fords—if they waited, as he waited, for five o'clock. He thought the situation ridiculous, his waiting for someone to appear on the street and to walk along it. He had driven a hundred and fifteen miles. Why should he, like the others, sit behind a sheet of glass and wait? He had come a good distance to face a myth, a legend, and by God he would do it and not sit waiting.

He stepped down the worn treads of the stairway.

A young woman with a bulky parcel came out the door of the Big Store; ahead of her she herded a little girl with her knees, and she was saying, ". . . ever take you anyplace with me again." The child fled on ahead.

Harry Connard entered the Big Store, paused to get his bearings among fishing rods, creels and reels; rifles lay flat behind glass, and pocket knives and hunting knives. Hunting boots were arranged on counters; one stood upright and its mate still rested in a box. Here were the tools for modern man to follow in the steps of his ancestors, to stalk and to kill. A powerful, middle-aged man who had certainly stalked and killed spoke from the middle of the room.

"Will there be something?"

"I'm looking for the dry-goods department," Harry Connard said.

"Right through there."

Harry Connard passed through an archway into a woman's world. Three women stood close, murmuring as they lifted garments off a rack and held them before them, to get some idea.

"Well, maybe, but I don't think so."

"Makes me sort of look washed-out."

Overhead a wire basket scurried just below the ceiling and disappeared into a hole. Almost at once it emerged.

To Harry Connard's left stood a young woman behind a counter; it could be no other than she. He walked over. He paused. He stood quite still to express his presence. She looked directly into his eyes.

He said, "I'm Harry Connard."

There was no possibility she'd not heard of him. What she had heard did not much matter. That he didn't inquire about merchandise, or ask advice, that he simply spoke his name, must show her that he had come a hundred and fifteen miles to stand before her and speak his name. In short, he meant business, serious business.

"I'm Harry Connard."

She looked directly at him. "Yes?"

What he felt was exactly like drunkenness. But Harry Connard did not beat about the bush. He would say what another dared not. He asked the question that the man must still ask the woman.

She answered. He couldn't believe his ears.

"No," she said.

*

Later, Harry Connard could not account for the deep uneasiness that did not go away.

He had stayed in that hotel room and he had stayed alone. He had not touched a drop, either in public or where no one could see. He had spoken to one person and only to one person, and he remembered every moment of that encounter.

There was no reason why he should ever go back to Salmon.

And no reason why he shouldn't.

Chapter 11

When Zack Metlen returned from France he had no shoes to step into, except the army shoes on his feet. Clothes in those years might have been designed by someone who abhorred the human figure; army uniforms were especially hideous: wrinkled, bunching, hard to press. Zack's olive drab uniform hung on him. He wore the Signal Corps patch on his right arm, and a couple of ribbons on his chest, one showing he'd been attached to the Rainbow Division. Above his awful blunt-toed shoes, his trousers were cased in tough canvas puttees designed years ago for troops in India and meant to thwart striking snakes. There were no cobras on the Western Front, but military traditions die hard.

Zack knew he had no shoes to step into; that letter he had got. But not the one about his mother's death, and for weeks

John had been steeling himself to say what he had to say, face to face and without the screen of paper.

He was reluctant to pull the tarp off the big tan Locomobile and drive it to the depot; he no longer had a right to such a car. But he had promised to keep it safe for Zack. The car was a symbol of their last talk together and of a promise made. He drove it to the depot.

Zack was not the only soldier to return to that part of the country on that day. The others pushed ahead of Zack and ran into the arms of someone against whose breast they cried and murmured; into the arms of a mother who had read the casualty lists in the *Butte Miner* and had sometimes despaired that she would ever again lie awake worrying about her son's transgressions and his future. Two of the soldiers ran to girls who had doubted they would know again the shock of that searching penis and had lately been considering other arrangements.

John was not surprised that Zack was the last off; Zack did not push or hurry. He had a puzzling patience which John did not, and John knew he only partly understood what moved in the corridors of his son's brain. That there was probing and questioning there he did know. But not much more. Zack's patience was that of a man who had in mind some grand design; he had no need, as John had, to snatch at every luminous and ephemeral moment. John's only lasting prize had been Lizzie, who had vanished one morning between ten and noon when the winter sun had just touched the corner of the hospital.

Zack was grinning. John's heart sank. *He doesn't know.* Zack thought his mother had stayed home to frost a cake, to put the last touches on his room, to double the boy's pleasure: first his father, then his mother.

"Pa!" Zack shouted, coming to him. "Good old Pa. I've got stuff ahead in the baggage car." He carried only a small black satchel. "How's my mother?"

John couldn't speak. He took his son in his arms, and let that speak.

*

Later. "You don't have to stay here, Zack. There's nothing here."

Zack was gentle. "I have to stay somewhere, Pa."

"You can look on here as a stopping-off place."

"I don't need to go anywhere, Pa."

"You'd be crazy to throw away everything because you thought you should stay." John bit his tongue. Because Zack had no more than he. Zack had only what he carried in the little black grip, the clothes on his back, the junk in his room, the box from the baggage car.

"Don't worry. I won't throw anything away by staying here. I figure what I've got will work here well as anyplace."

"It's just that a man's got to think first of himself."

"You bet. A man's got to think of himself first."

Neither of them believed a word of that.

*

Before the Great War, when many men rode horses, and many kings sat upon thrones, and the sun is remembered as brighter and the moon more often full, a young man who some thought to be a little bit crazy discharged an electrical condenser, and caused a spark to fly from pole to pole. He noted that in the basement, three floors below, iron filings in a glass tube had been disturbed.

Then it might be that not only a wire or cable but the very air—maybe the earth and sea as well—would carry signals. And that was true. First the wireless telegraph, and then the wireless telephone.

"Before I got over there," Zack said, "the French used motorcycles and dogs to carry messages. But soon both sides dug trenches. That stopped the motorcycles, and the dogs might stop and make friends with the enemy.

"The British used homing pigeons, carried them to the Front in wire cages, and taped messages to their legs and turned them loose, and they flew back behind the lines to their loft.

"By the time I got there, the French and the British had strung wires up to the front, and they telegraphed. We Yanks strung wires up, too, but we didn't telegraph, we telephoned. They said we Yanks had the telephone habit."

John and Zack talked as men without women, never of lost schoolbooks, of a child's need for a dog, of neighbors who have declared that a man's child is no fit company for his own child. They seldom spoke of food. They opened cans, and ate standing up; they carried their soiled clothes to the Grayling Steam Laundry; there was no reason to make their beds. They found each other good company.

"The Germans crawled out and cut the telephone wires?"

"You bet they did. And when our own outfits moved up, they'd get tangled in our wires."

"Kaufman—I wrote you about him—he and I were stationed near Cologne a few months before the Armistice, and we'd done some figuring. We figured if you get clicks out of a telegraph, wireless telegraph, the same force that moved the sounder on a telegraph would move the diaphragm of a telephone. Like a regular telephone, except no wires.

"We went to work, and before the Armistice, our side had a few telephones without wires. Kaufman and I had a lot to do with that."

"More coffee, Zack? Go on." John liked the idea of telephones coming from telegraphs. It was a pleasant idea, and proved that anything might be done, and that Zack could do it.

"At first," Zack said, "they only worked for a few hundred yards, but when the Armistice came, they'd work almost a mile. But that was the end of it. With the war over, nobody needed wireless telephones."

"I guess they wouldn't."

"Anyway," Zack said, "but what I want, what I wish I had, was a little shack a few miles out in the country. Not a place to live. Just a roof to keep equipment dry. Batteries. Rectifiers. I'd like to find a one-lung gas engine and a generator. Just a shack."

John perked up. "I know the spot," he said.

Late next morning they drove out past the hospital; five miles this side of Black Canyon they turned left and drove across the flats over what had been a wagon road, and was barely perceptible. It was a poor land that supported short, sparse sagebrush, lean jackrabbits and tiny gray birds that darted from bush to bush and hid in the short hot shadows of the advancing sun. Zack had folded down the top of the Locomobile, and out the back hung half a dozen pine two-by-fours. Ahead of them the sun beat down at such an angle that the heat waves enchanted the land ahead—it appeared to lie far under water. And once it did. A number of years back, three geologists had come there—two young ones and an old one—and they had stopped at John's hotel, and he had gone out there with them, and could talk to them because he'd read the article in the *Britannica* on trilobites. He had watched them—they were small against that horizon—searching with picks and shovels for shelled creatures forever fixed in stone, a reminder that all things pass and are succeeded by new creatures who will one day themselves be fixed in stone. What could it be, John wondered. To what ultimate conclusion did each expiring succession lead? Would there one day be a great rejoicing and the sound of music and laughter?

The abandoned log cabin lay just beyond a dozen acres that ten years before had been plowed for the last time. The land now resembled the face of a washboard, but the furrows had been so eroded by wind and rain that the car could easily have passed over them directly to the cabin. Even so, Zack turned the car suddenly to the right and approached the cabin as if the parched land were alive and green. John glanced at Zack, pleased. In so approaching the place, Zack was showing a nice respect for the failed effort of a dryland farmer.

The glass panes in the two small windows had all been

smashed, most of the glass inside on the buckled plank floor; stones had been hurled from the outside. No roving band of boys, in whom puberty stirs and whispers of the violence innate in man—no roving band of boys can abide the daylight playing on glass in an abandoned building. There may be few sounds so satisfying as shattering glass. Had he been such a boy? No. Had Zack? No. They were a couple of outcasts. It was something of a relief to admit it.

He felt tired. "I'll stay down here and encourage you," he told Zack, who was about to climb up on the sod roof and prepare to build something high.

"You're all right?"

"Fine. Just tired."

Above him began hammering and sawing. Zack's occasional footsteps were awesome with a disembodied quality, perhaps like the footsteps of a stalking fate. It was such ideas that often made John drift into reveries; if he'd been asked to explain what he was thinking, he couldn't have said.

The cabin smelled of desiccation and poverty. Of furniture only a stool remained; he sat on it and fixed his attention to a calendar on the wall, open to August 1909. The dark young Dane who had settled on the place had had no more than a plow, a harrow, and a team of horses, one or the other of which he used as a saddle horse, riding bareback, which no other white person in the state would have considered. It was overlooked that perhaps some people couldn't afford a saddle.

In 1909 the young Dane had plowed and harrowed and planted; but it did not rain. Often it had not rained. In August he shut the door behind him, leaving forever the pretty girl in the picture on the calendar, every man's girl before he married. The girl had just left off laughing; a smile lingered on her lips. She was driving an automobile, one lovely hand easy on the steering wheel. Say a word, and she would laugh again. The windshield was folded down, and the breeze swept back her blond hair. She was a peach. To the young Dane, a failure, she was as remote as her automobile—of uncertain make, since you saw only the wheel, a little of the dashboard, and the windshield.

But up there on the wall, she had meant hope, because such girls exist, and it was only a picture he'd shut behind him, and he was young, and strong, and there are many, many better jobs than dryland farming, and his time—like Zack's—must come. But with so little certain, the fall of the rain, the turn of a card, the next heartbeat, didn't every man deserve to love before he was fixed in stone?

Chapter
12

"You are all a lost generation."

Ernest Hemingway and others took comfort in Gertrude Stein's remark; it gave them license to refuse responsibility. Among the lost were many young men besotted by the new toy, radio. The world called them hams. They had no interest in what they sold or built or lifted; they didn't care what was going on at the shop. They countenanced the necessity of the day because, for reasons not yet understood, reception was best at night, and as the sun moved off toward the Pacific, zone by zone they flicked their switches, turned their knobs, and their real life began again. The rigs they hunched above, the grids, tubes, resistors, meant nothing to them; what counted was the platitudes they would hear from the fellow several miles away, and for that they waited, rapt as monks over manuscripts.

Be charitable: they could have done much worse. Ham radio was a lot cheaper than booze or tramping around Spain.

*

Zack Metlen and Bill Kaufman wanted a lot more than that, and meant to have it. There were obstacles, but although Zack was not the sort to say so, he thought he could do his part. No. He knew it. The trouble was that his part wasn't enough without what Bill could do. Maybe that's why when the letter came, he didn't open it. Instead, he left it in his room, where the clear cold north light glinted on his sending and receiving rig, a mess of wires and batteries incomprehensible except to him, and went about the business of his day.

But he found himself thinking a lot about Bill Kaufman, who was supposed to market what Zack made.

In the Signal Corps he had liked the man from the first—well, almost from the first, because Kaufman had begun with one remark that Zack would never have made.

"My father's a chiropractor," Kaufman said. "He meant to be a doctor, but he never made it."

What does a man make of such frankness? Zack had said only that his father was a rancher.

"So I guess it's up to me to make it," Kaufman said.

However, he had misinterpreted a few things Zack had said about the ranch, mostly, Zack guessed, to remind himself that there had been more in his life than howling shells and lice. He had spoken of the big herds, the rolling acres, the green fire of his mother's rings on the keys of the black piano.

"Your father sounds like a rich man," Bill Kaufman said.

Zack could not bring himself to say, "He has lost all of it."

*

In 1888 a young German named Hertz had identified radio waves, and a little later, in England a Professor Lodge caused a bell to ring across a clubroom: neither of them realized what they had done. It was Marconi who realized what commercial wonders were now possible, who hired attorneys and got rich. And it was not until one evening when the fog lay thick, the air silent and moist with death, that Zachary Metlen saw what, from radio, could come next.

Zack rose from the bed of an army truck when an American officer appeared out of the fog to hand him an envelope, endorsed with the proper signature.

"Please get this through at once."

Turning the crank of his wireless telephone, he was to call across a mile of dead and bloating horses, in code, of course, AURORA WANTS TO KNOW IF ELGIN IS ON THE OTHER END. He picked up his headset, snugged it over his ears, expecting to hear that faint throbbing that pulses when the ears are stopped—what a child hears from a seashell. But what he heard was something else. No, heard is not the word. Rather than sound there was a presence, an expectant void, as when the sustaining pedal of a piano is depressed and the felts raised from the strings. The circuit on the other end was open, the receiver off the hook, so to speak. What was surprising was that there was no noise, no static, no pops and cracks: only that strange, waiting presence.

And then, exactly as if he sat in his room at the ranch and listened, across the ryegrass, to some lonely fellow in the bunkhouse, he heard the paper-thin wail of a harmonica.

It was the clarity of the sound that astonished.

For those few moments, at least, radio was perfected.

*

When supper is over, when you've brushed up the crumbs and wiped out the frying pan, you have to read your mail. That's how it is. Whether or not your friend has written what you want to hear, he has the right to say what he needs to say, and you the duty to hear him out. Zack climbed to his room. Bill Kaufman's letter began as you'd expect from a friend.

Friend Zack!

When you got back I guess you saw the Statue of Liberty but I saw the Custom House Tower from Boston Harbor. It hadn't changed. Neither has State Street, where's there's a lot of money around that we aren't going to get. That little black music box has got to be clear as a phonograph, or the Big Money says no.

And anyway, if our pipe dream about a little black box in every house came true, the fellow who'd profit is the one who invested. I don't have the dough to form the company and hire lawyers and talk to bankers and congressmen. Do you?

I've got a girl who says she doesn't want much but me. We go out this week to see if we can find half a double-decker in Dorchester. That's what people do. Zack, who amounts to much in the Big Picture?

Zack folded the letter carefully and slipped it back so neatly into the envelope that it might never have been received or read.

Then he went down to where John was wondering where he was and said, "Pa, I've got to get a job."

"Not a bad idea," John said. "Doing what?"

"Damned if I know."

They both started laughing. "I never knew either, Zack. Funny how some men know exactly what to do." And he thought to himself, Your mother once said I ought to have been a poet. She said, "Poets live." But sometimes I get sort of scared.

However, you don't talk that way. Not to your son.

So John said confidently, "Whatever you turn your hand to, Zack, you'll do just fine."

Chapter
13

The Program Committee of the Pioneer Days celebration across the Continental Divide in Salmon, Idaho, sent copies of the special edition of the *Recorder-Herald* over to Grayling some days before the festivities that would take place on July Fourth. A copy fell into Zack's hands the night before the celebration, a hundred and fifteen miles away. The paper listed what might be observed or enjoyed, a three-legged race for adults, a sackrace, target shooting, a display of early firearms, fireworks arranged by a professional, and a *tableau vivant* on the island under the new bridge that had replaced the old, scary one—and that was the reason for so lavish a celebration. A ribbon was to be cut. Of the nature of the *tableau vivant,* so little was written that it was suspected that somebody might have a surprise up his sleeve.

For Zack, the celebration was no more than a sad little

reminder that celebrations are for people who have something to celebrate, and he had not.

However, an outsider had bought space in the *Recorder-Herald*, announcing that he would be in Salmon a week, and could be reached in his rooms at the Shenon House as late as noon on the day of the celebration. He would interview young men who were live wires for positions as Commission Merchants for reasonably priced electric light generators. This opportunity no aggressive young man should miss; this opportunity was looking him right in the face. The man signed himself Mr. Roscoe Cornell. The title Mr. was not much used in that country, and that he was taking rooms instead of a room made it clear that he was used to commanding more space that most people can afford.

Was Zack a live wire? But he couldn't think of another man who was better qualified to sell electrical equipment, and there was a demand for what he would sell, as Mr. Roscoe Cornell must very well know. The outdoor privy and the kerosene lamp were seen as the last relics of the Dark Ages. Women, especially, from the very beginning had been apprehensive about the open flame and would welcome electric lights out there in the country distant from the power lines. It was not the earthquake that so destroyed San Francisco. It was kerosene lamps and the fires that followed.

And Zack found something attractive in the serendipity of having picked up the newspaper exactly when he did, so shortly after realizing he was going to have to get a job of some kind. It was something in the order of "Ask, and you shall receive." Like his father, he more than half believed in signs and portents. How can one not believe, in a world where the astonishing might happen, and does?

He left Grayling at seven in the morning, having in mind the possibility of punctures, and understanding that the road over the Divide was so poor that twenty-five miles an hour was a good average, even for a Locomobile. But he would be there in good time before Mr. Roscoe Cornell had checked out. As he drove, he felt a pleasant warmth toward Mr. Cornell steal over him, and he saw Mr. Cornell as an older man, maybe even a gray one, who had had a son in France, and that in itself would be a bond between them. Certainly from such a man Zack might expect kindness and consideration, so that Zack might suggest that he choose his own territory right there around Grayling so that he could be with his father. Cornell would certainly understand that, wanting his own son near him, as he did.

It had not from the first occurred to Zack to telephone ahead to the Shenon House. Why should it have?

Zack did better than twenty-five miles an hour, and arrived in Salmon just past eleven. He pulled up before the Shenon House.

The Shenon House did not seem to be a very well run hotel. No one was behind the desk when he walked in, and no one was in the lobby—understandably enough on the day of the celebration. On the desk beside the register was a nickel bell to lay your palm on if you needed anybody, and Zack laid his palm on it. A young man appeared from out of a doorway that must have led into the bar.

"Do anything for you?"

"I've come to see Mr. Roscoe Cornell."

"Who?"

"Isn't a Mr. Roscoe Cornell here? Registered here?"

"Registered here?" The young man flipped through the pages of the ledger that lay on the desk. "I don't see him here. I never heard of him."

Zack was sick with disappointment, and even anger. He felt the butt of some awful joke, some hoax. But a good deal could have happened between the time Mr. Roscoe Cornell had the advertisement put in the paper and the present moment. Maybe he'd gotten sick. Or someone in his family had disappeared, or gone crazy. But however it was, he wasn't here.

"Thanks," Zack said, and walked out into the sun. Lord, how he had hoped. And how sick he was of hoping. Sick of hoping, he stopped in at the Pony Café across the street and ate a ham sandwich. From there he drove over across the new bridge and parked the car. There was no shady spot. Still sick of hope, he walked down the steps on the bridge to the island where everybody was, celebrating, and he the bystander.

*

In Grayling, John had arcane business to attend to. Zack gone, now was the time to do it.

When John had lost the ranch, when the manager of the hotel left, John wished him well. John's bitterness was not directed at his manager. The man couldn't be expected to work for nothing. And what he felt wasn't bitterness, because bitterness comes from a wrong done a man, and no man had done him wrong. He had failed because of a winter, and of his own foolishness. What he felt was self-pity.

When that manager had gone, John locked the back doors of the hotel, the side door, and the cellar door, and finally the big front doors. He called a handyman, who came with lumber, and boarded up the tall first-floor windows so young people wouldn't smash the glass to get inside and mingle with the ghosts there, and light candles, and make love.

John had wanted never to enter the building again. Except for it, he might still own his own land. But he had no sooner drawn the key from the last lock than he was struck by a certainty that he'd left something behind. He glanced at the key in his hand, considered going back in, and didn't. Since he couldn't account for what he'd lost, how could he look for it?

When he had told Lizzie that he had locked the doors, she had made a practical suggestion. "Somebody will buy the chairs and tables and beds, and the pots and the pans and china and the stove."

He had not thought at all about such things.

"And even the curtains and the old spittoons," she had finished. "Junkmen come around."

He had not been able to go back for the little money,

because he knew that what he would really be looking for was some part of himself. And that was crazy. But now his son was back and needed every penny they could raise. So to go back once more and look through the old rooms would be wise, wouldn't it? Even provident.

And not crazy.

*

John knew that when you are going to do something only after somebody leaves, it's a wise thing to wait a little while; somebody might come back because he's forgotten something and catch you doing what you were going to do. So John didn't walk down to his hotel until he thought Zack a good ten miles out of town.

Then he picked up the keys from a drawer. Going back to that hotel was painful. Maybe it was mad. John had seldom considered suicide but often thought himself a bit mad. However, he had come to terms with the man he'd locked inside down there—himself. That might not be a sane way to feel, but it was what he felt. And what he did when he got back inside—well, a court of law would have packed him off to the asylum at Warm Springs.

The asylum at Warm Springs was a showpiece of the state; it could be mistaken for the main hall of any college campus. In the summertime the big lawn was well tended and from white flagpoles, circled round with whitewashed stones, Old Glory flew and the state flag of Montana—a pick and shovel, a plow, mountains in the background, and underneath the state motto: Oro y Plata. To one side of a sedate red-brick building was a grove of cottonwoods—a little park, where people walked or sat on wooden benches. The women were dressed alike in forest-green housedresses and the men in clean overalls. It was a peaceful scene except for an occasional screamed obscenity that made clear the business at hand and the reason for bars on the upper windows. These people exist and are the state's responsibility. They are only we, damaged.

As a state institution, Warm Springs was open to the public, and groups from high schools and colleges drove over if the weather was fine to see how the state did things. The students were chaperoned by unsmiling teachers who wished to believe this outing was not an outrageous invasion of privacy. It was best to bring along a lunch and to picnic along the road, for although it was possible to eat at the cafeteria in the asylum and observe the inmates eating, the odor of baked macaroni and meat loaf was sickening. After a visit to Warm Springs, many young people whose lives were ahead of them, whose fathers and mothers loved them, who played games well or musical instruments and realized that soon they were going to fall in love—many young people vowed they would never again eat macaroni.

Once at the asylum, they had to go through with their visit. They had to file behind their chaperons into the wards past beds where eighteen-year-old boys had to be changed like babies; where old women cooed at rag dolls and gaunt old men picked from their flesh imagined filth. The students filed silently, shocked by groans from behind closed doors; they recalled stories, too often repeated to be groundless, of inmates beaten by male nurses who had stood all they could stand. And who was to blame the nurses? They were poorly paid; they had no status in the community. A consideration of one's own violence was inevitable, and of a father's, even a mother's violence. The students remembered things they had overheard, and oh, what a relief it was to be out under the big sky again and into the car and on the way to home.

*

It was around noon when John went into his hotel to find himself. Someone impatient for glory had set off a string of firecrackers at the far end of the street, and dogs around town, mistaking the racket for gunfire, barked and howled— surely jackrabbits were dropping in their tracks somewhere near. Under the cover of all that commotion, John thought it likely that no one had noticed when he entered his building.

The sunlight behind him wedged through the open doors to reveal the reception desk and the cubbyholes where the room keys lay; he located the light switch beside the heavy door that led to the stairway up into the tower and touched the button. No lights went on. Of course not. Responsible to the end, his manager had thrown the main switch when he left. John had no idea where that switch was. Well, then, there were candles in the rooms upstairs.

In its last days, the hotel had kept only six rooms open and made up, and three of those were seldom occupied. For fanciers of hotels, Grayling was a town to bypass; no one nowadays cared to go down the hall to a bathroom; a fire escape is a better means of fleeing flames than crawling down a rope. In each room stood a commode, pitcher and basin above, chamber pot below, there for a generation loath to count on waiting until morning. The second-floor windows had not been boarded up. They were translucent with a year's dust, and two generations of houseflies had bumped futilely against the glass. Most now lay dead on their backs; a few still struggled. From each room John took a candle and a holder.

Downstairs in the barroom, he struck a match, lighted one candle and set it on the end of the bar. From it he lighted the five remaining candles and arranged them a yard apart along the dusty mahogany; the reflected flames leaped like fireflies among the bottles lined in tiers on the back bar. Above and behind them, Custer made his last stand; the slightly wavering flames played on the texture of the painting and brought it life. Custer stood knee-deep in dead and falling friends, and innocent, expiring horses tangled on their sides.

Custer's eyes showed him to be clearly mad. His hat was entirely lost and his fashionably lengthy locks were swept aside by a powerful wind. His pistol, spent, drooped useless in his right hand.

John moved behind the bar; he picked up a whiskey glass, chose a bottle. Not one of those bottles would be legal much longer in this country. He poured the drink and set it on the bar. Then he came around to the front of the bar, put his foot up on the rail, picked up the glass and raised it. He spoke aloud.

"Custer, here's to you. Here's to you, George Armstrong Custer."

And he downed that drink. Again he went around behind the bar and poured himself another drink and went back to drink it. He spoke aloud again. "Custer," he said, "we were vain, desperate and foolish." He downed that drink and wiped his mouth. "Both of us."

And he knew someone stood behind him.

He took his foot from the brass rail and turned slightly; if no one was there, he had not given himself away by turning completely. And he could not be absolutely sure.

But someone was there, and it was a woman.

"Looks real pretty all lit up like this," she said. "I'm Lucille Talcott."

It was a voice that touched no string of memory; not an educated voice, but that had little to do with anything: and all Montana voices sound the same. Lizzie, however, would not have said "real pretty." "Attractive," maybe. Maybe "unusual." But although he thought he'd never before heard the voice, he had a strong impression that he'd seen this woman somewhere and in a riveting context, seen her, but at a remove—as if glimpsed briefly in a mirror. Or was it exactly the face a man expects when he is caught at something, as he had been caught at a bar talking to a picture and with candles all around?

She stood beside him and he moved to make room for her, as if strangers crowded them on either side. Never before had he stood at a bar with a woman.

She wore a dark suit Lizzie would have described as "fitted," and she was a bit too heavy. As a woman—that half of humanity privileged to defy, with makeup, time, weather, and the pull of gravity—well, she was good-looking. A man wouldn't mind being seen with her. But he doubted that she was much younger than he, and he doubted that her hair had once been so truly red.

"I was having a drink," he said.

"Yes, you were." She smiled.

"Would you have a drink?"

"I don't mind if I do."

He smiled and walked around the bar and served her. He came back around and stood beside her. She wore a pleasant scent. She sipped her drink and didn't shudder. "I drove down from Butte," she said. "I live in Butte, now."

She seemed to take for granted that he knew where she had lived before. Where had she lived? Like a hawk, his mind hovered over dozens of restaurants, a score of hotels. Had she been a waitress, a chambermaid? If so, she seemed to have come far. He'd always gotten on with waitresses and they with him; nothing serious, you understand, but there was a sauciness about their hand-to-mouth lives that appealed to him and made him liberal with tips. People don't know how much waitresses count on tips. He talked to them about their children, looked at snapshots and once—oh, he remembered that awful time—had promised to pray for one of them. He, whose prayers had never amounted to a damn.

"I saw you come in here and I wanted to talk to you. To talk business."

Ah. That accounted for her dark, fitted suit that was meant not to distract. But what business? "A bar's a good place for that, Miss Talcott."

"Well, it's the bar I want to talk about. I want to rent it."

For a second John's heart leaped. Money. But his heart subsided. He had taken her for a capable woman, one who considered and moved only after that consideration.

"I'm afraid you're a little late, aren't you?" he said.

"You've made other arrangements, then. Unless they're final, I can pay you five hundred dollars a month. Cash."

Five hundred a month—cash! A man and his son could live on that.

"Miss Talcott, I have no other arrangement. I'm not much

good at arrangements. Five hundred dollars a month looks big to me. Awfully big."

"Good. Do we shake hands?"

John's smile was sad. "You read the newspapers, Miss Talcott?"

"The headlines, yes."

"Then you know it's all up with liquor, first of the year."

"That's what they say."

"Then I don't understand why you would want—that's if you understand the situation."

"I understand the situation, Mr. Metlen. Completely." She smiled, touched his arm, and he was aware of her scent. Roses? "Mr. Metlen, would you please go around and pour us another drink? This one's on me. I have five hundred dollars right here in my purse."

He turned for a moment so she couldn't see his face. "A lady never bought me a drink before."

Her laugh was comfortable. She said, "A lady. Thank you for that, Mr. Metlen. But I thought you'd recognize me."

"Miss Talcott, I had a funny feeling that I did. I went back over things."

"I think not far enough, Mr. Metlen. You see, you were there when your wife stepped off the pavement and picked up my purse." She raised the new drink toward him.

Then she said, "That's what I call a lady."

Chapter
14

"Pioneer Days" are common now in Western towns, and organized not only out of respect for the past but to give people a chance to dress up and act as their fathers and grandfathers did. Only a rare man in the West knew much about his grandparents. In the West, they had no example of truly remote ancestors. In the East, descendants dressed like Pilgrims and walked to Plymouth Rock, heard speeches by the governor, by the Unitarian minister, and by one or two true descendants of Carvers, Saltonstalls and Howlands. In the East they thought long thoughts of storms at sea, of cruel winters, of hunger and marauding Indians. Many a baked bean was eaten, many a fish cake, and thanks given.

In the West, the regional Saltonstall was some fellow who first ran across gold in a stream, arrived with a herd of cattle,

or even set up a dry-goods store. They, too, had their marauding Indians. A few forefathers in the West achieved
importance because they had been accepted by the Indians.

The first celebration in Salmon was conceived early in
1919 to allow time for the growth of beards; one man's beard
may not fulfill itself so quickly as another's. The beards were
meant to honor forebears, but some men of forty had never
seen the true faces of their fathers. The true faces of their
fathers were somewhere behind stiff sheltering fur; since the
facial muscles of their fathers that registered anger or joy or
sentiment were hidden, and only by the look in a father's eye
might be known the present nature of his disposition, it is
small wonder many men had grown up thinking of their
fathers as inscrutable. Here now was a chance to wear a
beard and to appear inscrutable to wives and children, and to
see if that made any difference. Wives and sweethearts pro-
tested that beards scratched and that food caught in them.
Some wives may have felt a privacy invaded, for a husband's
beard declared something of the nature, texture and pile of
a man's pubic hair. Maidens wondered.

Pioneer Days were to begin on July Fourth with the firing
of a Civil War cannon hauled out by railroad some years
earlier as a centerpiece for the lawn before the new courthouse. It was an appropriate symbol of justice, whose de-
fender it had been, but no one knew exactly how to use it;
people glanced and walked past it. It was silent and threat-
ening: justice about to speak.

The chief event would be the opening of the new bridge
over the river. It had been completed some weeks before and
all had crossed many times with no ceremony whatever, but
on the Fourth a red-white-and-blue-striped ribbon was af-
fixed across both ends of the bridge. The ribbon would be
cut by the mayor on one side and the postmaster on the
other, and then those traveling across it in opposite direc-
tions could smile as they passed, and wave.

On the Fourth, the women wore dresses and bonnets of
forty years before; on their porches, a few serious ones dis-

played candle molds, churns and tinware made by grandfathers. Few men wore ancient raiment. It's the women's clothes that get saved. But the change in men's clothing is glacial, and it was the beards that counted.

It was decided not to shoot off the cannon; curiously, what had seemed a capital idea no longer seemed so. Someone recalled that during the Civil War cannons had frequently exploded, the barrels bursting into lethal fragments that killed some who might otherwise have died for a cause and, so to speak, on purpose. Furthermore, unless the cannon was removed from its poured-concrete foundation, a ball fired from it might well drop directly on the home of a man named Edwards whose brick house was the largest in town. So it was decided that a dozen men, sons of pioneers, should fire a dozen venerable Winchester rifles into the air at a given signal from the courthouse steps, a more appropriate salute, come to think of it, than a blast from a Union cannon. There were still men in town with Southern sympathies.

At eight in the morning of the Fourth of July, 1919, the sky clean and blue, the Winchesters were fired and the celebration began.

When the noon siren in the firehouse wailed and dogs all over howled at what they regularly took to be the voice of a dangerous intruder, the ribbons on the bridge were cut with new scissors, and people drove and walked across, conscious of history. In the middle of the new bridge, concrete steps led down to an island in the river; it lay like a ship-shaped raft. Until now it had been the domain of boys not yet seized by puberty. From the old iron bridge they had swung down to it on knotted ropes and might have fallen to their deaths, but they had not. In the summer when the water was low, they had directed log rafts at it and the current had carried them across. They might have been drowned, but they had not been.

On the island they built houses in trees; they could see everything through the branches and nobody could see them. Even the most determined enemy could not get them. They were prepared to rain rocks on his head and to run him through with wooden swords. They worked with hammers and stolen nails, with bits of lumber spirited off by night from the lumber company, and with small beached logs. They worked as fiends work, dismissing cuts and bruises and blood blisters—these who at home would whine and complain if asked to lug a pail of drinking water or a stick of firewood. High up in the trees they smoked cigarettes and tried chewing tobacco, and they threw up. They decorated the tender undersides of their forearms with skulls and crossbones, and dug holes in the earth and buried treasures of marbles: glassies, agates, flints, and chinks; sometimes also bits of money, pennies and even nickels; and they drew maps to show where these dear possessions might be located in time to come if, say, a person died of a terrible disease or had to move away with his parents to where there were no friends and where nobody knew him. But now, alas, the island belonged to everybody, and especially to grown-ups.

To the town, the island was a pretty piece of reclaimed land, and plans for it were afoot. There would be benches where those weary of the sight of their parlors and of the everlasting bulk of the upright piano against the far wall might sit of an evening and enjoy the murmur of the water in the river and hear the clear call of the killdeers. But today the Masons and the Elks had set up tables of raw pine planks, and the Order of the Eastern Star and the DAR and perfectly decent women with no such qualifications laid out white tablecloths and fried chicken, potato salad, baked ham, Van Camp's pork and beans, pickles and corn relish and freshly baked rolls. Near the water, where the women had required the men to build the fire, lest the flames get away from them and set the whole island ablaze, the men placed gallon coffeepots over the coals as they had learned when young, hung from two forked willow sticks with a straight stick across them.

Moving daintily on the periphery of this serious business, unmarried girls whispered, soft and pretty in fluttery summer dresses. Not for them those dowdy garments of another age that their mothers had dragged out of shabby trunks and laid in the sun to remove the stink of mothballs. These young ladies were no help at all: their minds were on the young men who joked among the trees. The past is all very well, but it doesn't have much to do with the future.

Their elder sisters could have told them a thing or two. They, too, the elder sisters, had but recently worn ribbons, and they knew where ribbons led—to washtubs and diapers, to whimpering children, to sudden rages and slammed doors and reconciliations, and offering yourself at night to a man if he had the mind to take you.

Apart from the other young ladies stood Anne Chapman. She wore white in compliment to the season, but as many said, it didn't matter what she wore, since a light played about her; that light was impenetrable as a wall, and so it had been with her since she was hardly twelve years old. At about that time, on the playground, the boys, in awkward but skilled maneuvers, would stand between her and the other girls and, as if she did not exist, they would run and punch one another and grunt. They rolled and tumbled and wrestled quite near the light around Anne Chapman, hoping she might gather that in time to come such exertion, such grunts and the ability to pin down another boy, foreshadowed the man who would uproot the forests, dam the rivers, build the railroads, tear down the skies and cast them at her feet, if that's what she wanted. What began as a scuffle sometimes became a battle; the wrestling got serious; there were gaspings, chokings and sometimes blood. The victor, his knees planted hard on the chest of the boy beneath him, hoped that Anne Chapman took note.

Other little girls stood fascinated at this dire masculine performance. The minds of boys were unfathomable; boys were a race apart. Ah, but it was hateful that boys alone had the right to choose, and hateful whom they chose. Of Anne Chapman the girls whispered.

"And who does she think she *is*?"

And so speaking, they felt better. Because they knew exactly who she was: she was part Indian. Suppose *they* had been born part Indian? But they were not. They should worry, they should care, they should marry a millionaire.

Yes, the grandfather had married an Indian. She was now dead. Anne Chapman and the old man lived in a small house on the edge of town. The old man had a few dairy cows, and brought the cream to the creamery in a neatly painted spring wagon.

A pretty girl is not expected to do awfully well in school; her superior social life naturally interferes with her studies, and anyway, one cannot have everything. Bright girls are not expected to be pretty. That is fair.

But it was not perceived as fair that Anne Chapman's marks in school were superior, certainly not by some of the mothers. What mother would wish a daughter to feel inferior to an inferior person? But mothers, who knew well enough what was unfair, also knew that unfairness, like a dead cat, can be laid at another's door.

"I'll tell you what I think," a mother remarked. "I wouldn't be surprised, not at all surprised, if the teachers were particularly kind to Anne. Don't you see, they feel sorry for her."

Now there is no greater pleasure sometimes than being able to feel sorry for somebody.. Then you have the upper hand. But it was hard to continue to feel sorry for Anne Chapman.

She was chosen valedictorian. Alas.

*

In 1916, when she was graduated, there were forty-three seniors; they sat in gray caps and gowns on folding chairs in the two front rows of the new gymnasium. The lectern was set on the collapsible stage that might be removed to allow more room for games and dancing. On one side of the stage were two chairs: one for the principal, one for the mayor. The Episcopal minister sat on the other—the Gospel—side.

The mayor, his legs crossed comfortably, was observed to

rock one congress-gaitered foot; he would be glad for the ceremony to start. He was an old hand at this. The principal's feet were firmly on the floor, the left one thrust somewhat forward; leaning on it, he would find himself nearer the lectern when his time came.

The Episcopal minister had not been seen on the stage for some four years; he had been preceded by the Methodist minister, the Baptist, and the Congregational. The Roman Catholic priest had never been approached; his congregation was recent and small. He met it for services in the storeroom above the Idaho Hardware Company, where boxes had been shoved against the wall to accommodate the Mass. To that echoing upper room he carried in a black valise his special clothes and the cups and serving dishes and napkins necessary to the sparse feast. None of his parishioners had finished high school, some had never begun; things of the mind were not for them.

The Episcopal minister, like the mayor, had crossed his legs, and so expressed an ease typical of his sect—a relaxed discipline that allowed a man to move with cheerful confidence through the terrors and pitfalls and humiliations of this life into the next with never a backward glance. He did not, as the mayor did, rock a foot upon an ankle, for he understood the nature of eternity. Eternity will not be hurried.

The principal rose and walked to the lectern; he smiled down upon two hundred heads and took a step back and one forward.

"Welcome," he said, "to one and all. Mr. Burgess will pronounce the invocation. Following that, we will hear from our salutatorian."

There was some creaking of folding chairs and some whispering—"salutatorian" is an uncommon word and not always understood in all quarters.

"And after that, from our valedictorian." And here the principal sternly swept the audience with his eyes.

He himself thought it more seemly when the valedictorian was male, and had so explained to the overwrought parents of the young man who had expected to assume that place. It is the man, after all, who hews the wood and brings home the bacon. Again and again it has been observed that the occasional bright young woman is liable, at times, to think herself superior to her husband; no good at all comes of that. Let those young women talk their French, arrange their flowers and paint their loaves of bread and their ripening fruit—but in the end, women lack discipline. How good it is to see a young woman holding a little child; in her tenderness and concern we see a confirmation of the future, toward which she has done all that is required.

Nevertheless, the hard facts were—and this was hard for them to understand and for the principal to explain—he who spoke first came second, and she who spoke last, first. And so the young man, and his father and his mother, had to settle for an honor that seemed to them womanish; because the principal, though limited, was an honest man, and grade points don't lie.

Oh, from the time he was in the first grade, it had been clear that the young man was headed for first place. He colored well within the lines, didn't crowd numbers on the paper, and if he erased, he did not lose his temper and damage the paper. Later his parents knocked on the door before they entered, afraid they might come upon him doing something too old for him.

Young friends were advised, "He won't come out just now. He's studying."

He was fair on the ballfield—not the best, but decent; he settled arguments in a firm quiet voice and was prompt for meals, though somewhat suspicious of strange food. A fine future was in store for him.

The ancient virtues were honored in those days, perhaps most honored in rural districts where the discontent brought on by poverty had not yet appeared, nor the wild crazy thinking. So when the young man rose from his slatted chair and mounted to the stage, he announced clearly if a bit sullenly, "My subject is responsibility." He spoke quite a long time.

Responsibility was a subject familiar to his audience. They knew how its practice impinged upon one's desires and comforts. It meant going without, that another might have. It meant sitting up, and being called on at strange hours. It meant keeping to yourself what might be cried out; it meant coming out of your room to face again God knows what.

It was remarkable that a boy so young was so acquainted with responsibility when he had not yet been tested. But on the whole his listeners were glad of him, glad that he had come from among them. Already he had been accepted at a university outside the state. If in later years he returned to town in triumph, having succeeded at something, they would welcome him and forgive his excellence.

A fine speech. The applause was sincere.

But the applause that followed the valedictorian's brief speech was spotty and hesitant. Full-bodied applause would have declared agreement, and there was hardly one among them who would wish his neighbor to think that he believed what the valedictorian hinted that she believed.

Anne Chapman spoke of God and Nathaniel Hawthorne.

In Salmon, Idaho, the tales of Hawthorne were associated with the odor of damp wool garments in the cloakroom, the hiss of chalk against the blackboard, and a Miss Scholtz, who had assigned *The Scarlet Letter* to her senior English class. Two girls had brought the fact to the attention of their parents. Miss Scholtz argued before the school board that the book was "literature," whatever that was, but it was removed from the shelves that year, and Miss Scholtz herself from the faculty the next.

But how times change: the young revolt and laugh in the faces of their elders, they wear masks and practice a secret life behind the backs of their elders; and it was not Anne Chapman's speaking of the tales of Hawthorne that was troubling, but her speaking of the tales of God. Now, no one in secular surroundings is comfortable with the name of God, except when an angry man will take His name in vain. It is only in sacred circumstance, within the walls of a church and surrounded by those whose very presence certifies their faith, that you are safe from the scoffer. Only there can you expose your naked need. Tell me this: where else is there to turn?

And now this schoolgirl stood before them with her unsettling presence, her witchlike beauty (Hawthorne, indeed!), and she seemed to say that if a Creator did indeed exist, He was indifferent to His creatures. In so speaking, she destroyed utterly what some desperately wished to believe.

It did seem that being part Indian was hardly punishment enough for Anne Chapman.

*

Three years later, that same girl stood on that island in the Salmon River, apart, and alone. And alas (a word that has quieted many a conscience), still unmarried. Until now she had had a good many beaux, and more than her share of little dances, birthday parties and taffy pulls, but Nature's plan for such merriment is that it end in marriage and in bed and—well, here she was, unmarried. And no great surprise, because when the cards are down, you have to think of a baby born. Who knew what part of a part-Indian mother the child might look like?

"Why, the kid might be born with black braids," a father remarked to a gloomy young man. "What about that?"

The young man's gloom was not relieved. He, among others, had courted Anne Chapman when he was fourteen, fifteen, seventeen, stinted and saved to buy her sodas and sundaes at the Red Cross Pharmacy, had inscribed her name deeply into his left forearm with a sharp pen and red ink; the wound became infected, festered; there were questions, hell to pay. Parents understand nothing. And then one day he looked at her and saw he hadn't a chance. She lived in a world apart, and he and those others were not going to enter it. But he would have accepted a child with long black braids and walked the floor with it because it was hers.

"Why," his father said, "you don't know how lucky you are she turned you down."

Oh, he knew all about his luck, all right.

*

Pioneer Days were unthinkable without *tableaux vivants* showing the arrival of the white man into the valley, and Miss Lowe of the English department was the very one to arrange them. She had spent two years at Emerson College in Boston, and there learned the Delsartian Method of elocution; she was known in Salmon for her scenes from Shakespeare, and she had worked with the lower grades on the Thanksgiving pageant.

The requirements of art having overcome those of modesty, she had made it clear to those who were about to appear that they must empty bowels and bladders before they went on stage, immobility being next to impossible if nature calls.

A small stage of raw pine had been erected, held together with a minimum of nails that it might be dismembered easily and the lumber put to permanent use. Bedsheets had been pieced together and dyed sky blue, that their parting might more closely resemble the parting of the heavens upon a scene in Salmon's past.

Bright sun dimpled the river; lunch was over and the women in their grandmothers' gowns moved quickly to remove and stack paper plates for later burning. The juice of canned baked beans soaks in, and limp, wet lettuce is nasty to the touch. Eating would be pleasanter without the aftermath.

From across the water came the explosion of the last firecrackers. The noise on the island, the laughter, the chatting and the yelping of the dogs moved closer to the small stage where very soon now people whom everybody knew were going to pretend to be somebody else. But among those who gathered around were some undesirables—what a shame it is that our world is pimpled by troublemakers. They move among us sneering at our arrangements and scoffing at our rectitude. They laugh, sometimes full in our faces, and many of them drink as well.

Among these was young Harry Connard, who had visited Salmon once before but at that time had given only one person any reason to remember him. Today he led a group who had driven over from Grayling, Montana, and although they would have been most welcome had they behaved themselves, they had not. They were first seen at the Owl Bar just as the parade, led by the high school band, began. Behind the band came, four abreast, local men riding saddle horses, and then came the new fire truck. As the band passed, it was disquieting to hear "Semper Fidelis" challenged by ragtime blaring from the bar. Shortly afterward, these troublemakers surged across the street to the Smoke House, carrying their drinks. From there they pressed down the steps from the new bridge to the island, and with the crowd they moved near the pine stage.

Society can deal with most troublemakers; when troublemakers overstep a certain line, they can be confronted by the authorities and carried away to jail, and there they can sober up and think. But the ringleader of this disturbing group was not one who could be shut in a cell beneath the new courthouse. He could not be treated as some might wish to treat him because he had the one thing that all people want, even though they pretend they don't want it, and pretend to have something of at least equal value—health, obedient children, a good name; but most people would trade whatever it was they said they had for what this man had, and that was money.

If such a man sees that you are forgiving of his escapades, he may later on view you with favor; your need and his resources may become one. He can be of help, especially when he owns a bank. But should you be one of those who laid a hand on him, his enmity will pursue you as far as rails run or wires stretch. He will bring you to your knees.

The folding chairs before the pine stage were there by

courtesy of the Elks, the Masons and the churches; men set them up and then stood aside to see that the rows were straight. Women do not like to unfold folding chairs; it is an awkward process and there is danger of pinching. Women dislike setting up folding chairs as men dislike carrying paper bags in public. The chairs began to fill up, and when they were full, a good many people stood or squatted to both sides and to the rear. Those rowdy ones were in the rear.

Those acquainted with theater manners through their attendance of the motion pictures at the Rex Theater began shushing to quiet noisier neighbors, but their "sh" sounds, blown around the tips of their tongues and through the front teeth, were directed particularly at the troublemakers. But troublemakers are only encouraged in their bad manners by efforts to silence them; they thrive on disapproval.

The sky-blue sheets billowed as the actors behind them took their places and so disturbed the close summer air.

The theme of the *tableaux vivants* could have been no other, in that country. It was that of the Lewis and Clark expedition that had passed nearby, guided by the Indian woman. The Western states were peppered with monumental invitations to remember this attractive trio. Hardly a dozen miles away beside a threadlike mountain stream—the true headwaters of the great river—was a cairn with a securely screwed brass plate inscribed with the words THANK GOD I HAVE LIVED TO BESTRIDE THE MIGHTY MISSOURI. In smaller letters, credit was given to Captain Meriwether Lewis, 1804. Over near Grayling, in Montana, another plaque urged one to consider the singular joy of Sacajawea when such memories as rise from dreams identified for her the very valley of her birth. Throughout the Rockies, the admiration for this woman was cultlike; her courage, her intelligence, her inaccessibility made her known to those who could not think of another Indian woman's name.

But when it was understood that Anne Chapman had been chosen to play the part of Sacajawea—doing just what, nobody knew, but certainly not being delivered of the baby by that Canadian trapper she had married during the expedition— some people were uneasy.

If Anne Chapman was going to play Sacajawea, it seemed strange that Miss Lowe, a gentle woman, would have asked her. It seemed even cruel that the girl publicly expose herself as Indian, what she might wish to be hidden. Those who had almost forgotten would be reminded, and it was particularly thoughtless of Miss Lowe to have chose the girl to play Sacajawea in the light of what was about to happen.

"Shhhh!"

Silence is the necessary background for *tableaux vivants;* it would not have done for Miss Lowe to part the curtains, come forth and break the spell with words. Therefore, when the curtains had reshaped themselves behind her, she held up a large white cardboard sign, the letters big enough for even the old to see. She held the sign slightly to one side so that she was herself visible in a long, cool chiffon gown of a silent gray.

CAPTAIN LEWIS RECEIVES HIS ORDERS.

The curtains parted.

President Jefferson sat sideways at his desk, every inch a President, one well-turned and gaitered leg extended. He, like the other actors in this scene, had had to forgo beards. Behind him, one hand lightly on the desk, stood his Vice President, Burr, whose foxlike face was fixed on the back of the President's head. A shorter man had been chosen as Captain Clark, since Clark was the junior member of the party and his true height lost to history; he was in cavalry uniform, wore his hat, and stood in a stiff salute.

Captain Lewis was taller; he, too, wore his hat, indicating he meant to let no grass grow under his feet the moment he seized the curling document the President held out to him. This curling document marred the scene a little; the slight trembling of the President's fingers was amplified in the receptive quality of the paper, and it all but waved. Observers of the actual scene, one hundred and sixteen years before, would remember it in hindsight as explosive. Before another year passed, Burr would have shot and killed Alexander Hamilton in a duel, and was himself ruined. It was rumored that the President with the well-turned leg had taken a black woman to bed. Captain Lewis reached the mouth of the Columbia River as instructed, and four years later killed himself. Clark disappeared from history.

The curtains closed. The audience had noticed no trembling lip, not a blinked eye; only that waving document disturbed the scene, and that may have been caused by a random breeze. There washed through the audience a sibilance.

". . . stand so still."

Undercover of this appreciation, Miss Lowe slipped back through the open seam of the curtains, and there was applause that died quickly to accommodate the next scene. Miss Lowe reappeared with a sign.

THANK GOD I HAVE LIVED TO BESTRIDE THE MIGHTY MISSOURI!

The curtains parted.

For this powerful scene, a narrow length of shiny blue cloth was laid from stage right to the center and tortured a bit to suggest running water; on either side were real bushes, both large and small, just gathered from along Jesse Creek. Their freshness was apparent to both eye and nose. One of the gatherers of those bushes had paused at her work and looked up into the empty July sky, astonished at the nature and variety of earthly chores.

Captain Meriwether Lewis wore the same cavalry uniform and the same broad-brimmed hat, but his shirt was torn from encounters with jagged rocks and wild beasts. In the best circumstances, a man can't travel from St. Louis to Montana without a damaged shirt. The captain's hands were raised to heaven, his palms open as if to receive something, his unblinking eyes fixed on the clean sky just above the railroad station beyond town. Straddling the narrow stream, he looked to the men in the audience as if he were, except for his closed trousers, about to urinate. There was that pensive look in his eyes. A lady—and maiden lady at that—Miss Lowe had posed him in all innocence, but there was hardly a man in town who had not at some time picnicked up there by the stone cairn on land now set aside by the government and named Sacajawea Park. Hardly a man who didn't know the insistent call of water in the narrow stream up there that burbled out from under a big shoulder, and many the time had straddled it. It was unthinkable that Captain Lewis, as he bridged the water, had not thoughtfully relieved himself into it, to make the mighty Missouri significantly his, just as the local boys had always done, consumed for a moment with the magnificence of history.

The curtains closed. But before they began to clap, somebody booed.

"Booo!"

It might have been a stone thrown. That boo was booed by one whose pleasure lay in spoiling the pleasure of others. In this life it is the boo that topples and destroys and shatters little dreams. It hung over the silence, an ugly dissonance.

People turned to look.

The man booed again. It was not surprising that he was contemptuous of Miss Lowe's efforts. Had she been of any account, she'd not have been teaching in Salmon, Idaho. The man who booed had had advantages closed to most people. As a boy he had traveled by Pullman to New York City for the opening of *The Red Mill;* he'd seen in Chicago the revival of *Mlle Modiste.* Real theater was as homely to him as was the Bible to these small-town folk. Had he not been drunk, he might have been amused by such amateurs; he would not then have booed. Some things must be forgiven a man if he is drunk, but it's hard to forgive a fellow who has hurt Miss Lowe's feelings and humbled the actors. From the first they had not been sure of themselves, had experienced qualms about exhibiting themselves in public, and had counted on the goodwill of their friends—the audience—to see them through. At the worst, their appearance as actors could later be regarded as a good-natured joke, or even community service—somebody had to help Miss Lowe with the country's history.

And it is not for nothing that the acting profession is looked down upon. It is a world of pretense, peopled by those who cannot fit in, whose feet are not on the ground, and who therefore can't be trusted.

The booing stopped, but the memory of it hung about like a stench, and when Miss Lowe appeared for the third and last time, the sign she held up trembled. But that lady had picked up from somewhere around Emerson College the laudable imperative that the show must go on, even as life itself, and she raised her chin. For this last scene, in its simplicity, she believed to be her triumph.

The trembling sign held up showed but a single word.
SACAJAWEA.

Without that Indian woman, the expedition from east to west might have failed; she had acted not only as a guide, but as an interpreter, and her traveling with the party had lent it a plausibility without which every man among them might have been scalped or murdered by Indians along the way. And miracle of miracles, shortly after recognizing the country of her birth, she and the party came across her own brother leading a hunting party, and he saw to it that they had fresh horses.

No drawing or painting from life existed of the woman; every man might make of her what he would. She had disappeared with her Canadian husband without a trace. She had the charm and the appeal of the remote, the vanished, the unattainable.

It was Miss Lowe's triumph to cast as the Indian woman the only one on earth (so far as she knew) who could play Sacajawea. Who could *be* Sacajawea. For over that young woman hung an aura of remoteness that matched one that the real Sacajawea had perhaps acquired only with the passage of a century. This remoteness, which had stunned the plain, unmarried Miss Lowe, was that which envelopes the absolute beauty, that unfortunate one whom many men don't dare approach for fear of rebuff, and who, because she doesn't want him, refuses that rare man who thinks well enough of himself to dare approach her.

The curtains parted, and there was Anne Chapman.

Her hair was in dark braids; she wore a fringed tunic of fawn-colored buckskin, met by elaborately beaded moccasins tall as leggings. She knelt on one knee, her astonishing face in profile, and with her right hand she shaded her eyes and looked into the distance—a classic pose, if a trite one. What the audience saw in that tableau had the appeal of certain pictures that they liked and hung on their walls—lithographs, prints that called to some emotion, struck some chord—a peasant girl looks up with rapture from the fields: "The Song of the Lark." Or a laborer toils under a darkening sky: "The Man with the Hoe." There was endurance for you.

In Anne Chapman's stillness on the stage, even those who seldom considered eternity had intimations of the everlasting. As an image, she was the difference between life and existence.

The curtains closed. The moment was similar to walking out of a matinee at the Rex Theater into the dusk and standing exactly where you had stood before you entered: a man was struck with a sense of loss. But was it loss they felt, or longing?

Struggling with the complex questions of the absolute and with the subtle connection between love and loss, the audience was not prepared for another booing, and there was none. But the same clear, drunken voice called out, "By God, a real squaw."

Then what happened happened so suddenly that many did not actually see it, and had to inquire closely later on.

"It was splendid," Miss Lowe was said to have said, and she may well have said it, because "splendid" was one of her words.

From the stage she had looked over the crowd and seen it all, and although she might have been expected to be startled by such unaccustomed violence, it was not expected that she would have been stirred in such a way. For "perfectly splendid" is actually what she said.

Because a young man had moved quickly forward and knocked the speaker to the ground. And he said, "If you get up, I'll belt you again."

In a few moments, when the assailant had moved away, the friends of the damaged man—they had stood apart like dogs anxious to see how things were turning out—approached and assisted their friend to his feet; they led him away. None of them was seen again that day. The editor of the *Recorder-Herald,* on hand to cover the *tableaux vivants,* had made notes for the next edition of his paper.

But the violent ending of the celebration never appeared in print, because of who the damaged man was. It is too bad that some men must be treated differently.

Few at the Pioneer Days celebration had ever heard a girl insulted publicly; having had no experience with so painful a scene and no proper understanding of it, they thought it best to ignore it. Surely it would be indelicate to try to comfort the insulted; nobody wants public pity, especially somebody who may deserve it. It was disappointing, an unpleasant end to an otherwise pleasant afternoon—see! there wasn't a cloud in the sky. But only the loose dogs on the island were oblivious to what had happened, and maybe the children, who were regularly exposed to the spectacle of violence on the playground and who hurled and received insults.

The crowd moved from the scene; the actors, except for Anne, left the stage.

*

Zack Metlen was now twenty-three years old; his sandy hair was unruly the moment the water on his moistened comb dried. He had powerful shoulders and an open face without a trace of guile, and about women he knew next to nothing.

In high school when it became quite clear to others that

there's a great difference between the sexes, Zack had missed out on the flirting and the passing of notes up and down the aisles and to the rear near the dictionary and the bust of Washington. His attention was elsewhere. He had accepted that girls got to giggle and did a lot to their hair, and that boys should excel at the more brutal sports; but none of this seemed applicable to Zack Metlen.

Nor did he understand the heroes of these girls, among whom one year was a young bandit who made off with a Waterman fountain pen. The pen was useless to the boy who owned it and to him who took it, since it was with a penholder and steel nib that all must write over and over again the word "Lanning" and the phrase "This is a specimen of my handwriting." The Palmer Method forebade the movement of the fingers; one was to slide and circle from the elbow, and the desired result was that everyone's handwriting should look the same. How, then, was a man to protect his check or his will?

The young hooligan was called into the principal's office and emerged smirking, to the ill-concealed admiration of several chattering girls. He had stolen the Waterman pen and been seen with it: but the proof had vanished. A man cannot be brought to justice without proof. Not in this country. To Zack, considering it at a later time, that admiration seemed to recognize cunning as a kind of power: Reynard the fox sheltered his vixen as the bear his sow. Hobbled by skirts, barely equipped to carry their own books, requiring the acceptance of some male before they could have any future; Zack had a lot of sympathy for girls and no interest in them. It did cross his mind that his mother was not at all like that.

But then, Zack's mother was different.

*

Mr. Roscoe Cornell having decamped or perhaps never having arrived, there was nothing else in Salmon City to engage Zack's interest. But the defection of Bill Kaufman was more troubling to him than he had expected it to be. If

Bill's belief could evaporate, perhaps the black box was, after all, only a dream and a diversion. In that case, what purpose was there to Zack Metlen? It was to postpone the long drive back to Grayling in the company of such thoughts that he had joined the audience before the small pine stage. He stayed because he saw at once that the performance would be amateurish. He knew that whoever put it on would hope that it would not be seen as amateurish, and it was out of a nudging sense of obligation to those who would try and most certainly fail that he sat there.

"You cannot," he had once heard his mother tell his father, "be responsible for the entire world."

But he knew exactly how his father felt.

At last the curtains opened on the final scene. Zack was bewitched. He watched that exquisite stillness in a trance, and the voice that cried out "Squaw!" was hideous as a man cursing a child.

Blinded by anger, he arose.

Ten minutes later, he stood near the steps at the side of the stage. At the bottom of the steps was a wiry old man in a turn-of-the-century suit, his haircut so recent that pale skin circled his skull below his black hat. The old man stood as his father was beginning to stand, not quite sure of his legs.

The old man in the old suit was looking up the steps to the stage. Perhaps no tragedies are singular, but Anne's grandfather had lost his wife to smallpox, once a selective killer of American Indians, and then his daughter to childbirth. How could this happen? The word "happen" is cruelly passive; it puts the blame on Nothing.

Then suddenly she walked down from the stage, the daughter of that daughter, and Zack saw them talking.

She was wearing a pretty summer dress, the braids were gone and her hair was all piled up, and there Zack was in his shapeless army shoes and army jacket, the worst color on a man, "shit brindle" they called it, and he'd begun to put on weight, because he and his father ate so much bread and potatoes.

The old man and the girl had seen him. And he had no words to explain his presence. For a second her eyes locked with Zack's. He didn't know that Socrates spoke of the Half that searches for the other Half that makes it Whole. But he did know that speech of some kind was required right now.

When you see people standing somewhere, you know they won't stay there long if that's not where they belong in the first place. Because they are going to want to go where they do belong, and so a man will say, "Can I give you a lift anyplace?"

Zack walked over. "I'm Zack Metlen. Can I give you a lift somewhere?"

"My name's Joe March," the old man said; they shook hands. "This is my granddaughter, and her name's Anne Chapman."

Zack no more than touched the girl's hand; his mother had once remarked that men didn't shake hands with women. Shaking hands, she said, began as a test of physical strength; there was no such test between men and women. And then the girl spoke to him, and said the most wonderful thing he'd ever heard.

"You are very kind." She might just as well have put her cool palm to his forehead.

He was just able to speak. "My car's on the far end of the bridge."

So they began to walk. The July sun bore down upon them from a cloudless sky. Because the day was fine, Zack had folded down the top of the Locomobile, and he worried that the leather seats would be too hot for comfort. He would lay out the lap robe for Miss Chapman; he and the old man must burn their legs and rear ends for a few minutes.

He was not happy about the make of the car. A young woman who has just been denounced publicly as an Indian and an old man whose granddaughter has just been so denounced would find small comfort in a car that represented the apex of the rich, white world closed to them.

Miss Chapman and her grandfather might fall silent at the sight of it. Old people often do just what they want to do; they have so little time left, they mean to arrange it to suit themselves, and Zack could imagine the old man's refusing to set foot in the car. He could think of no way, while they walked, to prepare them for the car. It gave a wholly wrong impression of his own circumstances; but just as he had failed to tell Kaufman about the Metlens' economic ruin, so he balked at telling this young woman that he was next to penniless. His army jacket and army shoes told the true story. Suppose they took his wearing army getup for a man bragging that he'd been Over There?

The old man stopped, and raised his head, and sniffed the air. "I smell rain," he said.

Anne paused. "A lot?"

"Yes. A big rain."

Not a cloud in the sky; the sun beat down. Why, the old fellow was making small talk. In small talk, one trivial remark leads to another.

"Not a cloud in the sky, sir."

"They come up," the old man said, "they come up, the clouds, there ahead."

"My grandfather is never wrong about rain," Anne said.

"I suppose I've been wrong," the old man said.

"Sir, we all have," Zack said.

The old man said, "I expect you haven't made many mistakes. You aren't old enough."

Anne said, "How good if our mistakes were only about weather. Grandfather, you shouldn't admit to making mistakes; Mr. Metlen will conclude you're a mistaken man."

Zack felt their close relationship excluded him.

Anne said, "I assume, Mr. Metlen, that you have made mistakes?"

Zack spoke seriously. What he said he felt to be absolutely true—true for the last few days. "My life has been a mistake."

"In the sense," Anne asked, "that you've gone in a wrong direction?"

"In the sense," Zack said, "that I thought there was a direction."

"Dreams," Anne said.

"He's not talking dreams," the old man said. "He's talking about direction. Let me tell you, young fellow, you're going in the right direction as sure as we're in for rain."

Zack had taken the old man's talk of weather as small talk, but he himself, in speaking of lacking direction, had suddenly turned the conversation serious.

"Remember what I say," the old man said. And he was serious.

Had the old man been an Indian instead of only being married to one, Zack might have half believed him. Indians talk with spirits and are aware of signs hidden from white men. And he couldn't understand anyway why he'd made so personal a confession to recent strangers. They must think the less of him for it. New acquaintances expect more reserve.

Of the enormous Locomobile, the old man said, "This is some big motorcar. Anne will sit in back where she can nod at people."

They lived at the edge of town, within easy walking distance of the bridge. They had no reason to accept a lift except to please him; if she'd been humiliated by young Connard's words, she'd have been less conspicuous walking home instead of riding slowly like royalty up the main street in a Locomobile.

Anne said, "Ah, how I should like to be rich and famous and ride about as if I were used to it."

That gave Zack the chance to make things clear. "I wish I had the right to drive this car."

"Naturally," Anne said, "when your people lost everything, they'd want to keep something for a souvenir."

"You know, then."

"Why pretend everybody in two states doesn't know what happened to the Metlens? Well-known people are at a disadvantage. It stirs the blood when famous people fall."

But he was not asked into the small brick house on the edge of town. It was established that he had nothing to offer. In consenting to ride with him, they were being kind to a fellow who had nothing else to give. The old man arranged his legs and got out of the car by himself. Anne waited until Zack came around to help her. They thanked him.

Zack said, "What I've wanted to say all along, wanted all along to say, is how much I enjoyed your performance."

Anne and the old man glanced briefly at one another; Zack wondered if they somehow took his remark as too personal.

Anne spoke. "What *I've* wanted to say all along, all along wanted to say, is how much my grandfather and I enjoyed your performance. My grandfather said your fist had a crisp sound when it landed."

"And what I've got to say now," the old man said, "is that since you've got this machine stopped, I'd put up the top and the side curtains."

There wasn't a cloud in the sky.

But to ignore the grandfather's suggestion was impossible. It was more than a suggestion, so to save the old man's face, he began the complicated business of enclosing the car. First the canvas cover had to be removed from the folded top. Then the top unfolded and pulled over the length of the passenger space. But where were the side curtains? They'd never been used. He found them in a neat recess behind the backseat, rolled up and stuffed into a canvas bag, and not easily removed, nor easily installed. While he was at this foolish work, two automobiles passed on the road and slowed. Both drivers had looked up into the clear, cloudless sky, and driven on.

"There's that bad spot at the bottom of the Hill," the grandfather said. "You might need your chains."

The old man and the beauty waved as he left; when he last looked into the rearview mirror, they still stood there.

When he'd driven a mile, he stopped the car and removed the front side curtains and tossed them in back. Anyone passing him would not then think him quite such a fool. He shook out a Fatima from a pack and lighted it; he stood a moment beside the car, about to remove the rear curtains and fold back the top. But he did not. He did not out of respect for an old man touched by age in a strange way, and "for a souvenir," as the girl had said, of that girl. He got back in the car and drove on.

Halfway down the Hill on the Montana side, a most astonishing thing happened. Bruise-colored clouds rolled up behind him, and lightning struck so close he smelled ozone. The rain fell in torrents. Human beings, like cats, hate getting wet; they carry umbrellas, they wear oilskins, they run for cover. Zack drove with one hand; he moved the windshield wipers with the other. Should he stop and put up the curtains? No, if he stopped for that, the rain would have time to create that mudhole and he'd have to get out and put on the chains.

He didn't get through the mudhole without chains.

*

"I was worried," his father said. "Haven't seen rain like this in a dozen years. You must have got soaked, putting the top up. Did you find the side curtains? Were there any?"

Zack didn't explain that he'd left the town of Salmon, Idaho, under a cloudless sky with the Locomobile fully rigged at the suggestion of an old man who believed himself to have powers of divination. It crossed Zack's mind that maybe the old man did have such powers. You read of such people, and although nobody believes in them, everybody does believe in them sometimes.

But however his father professed to have been worried, sunk in a mudhole with a broken axle—struck by lightning?— his father struck him as cheerful and animated. His father continued. "Well, the Loco got you through in good shape, we can say that for her. And now we can think twice about selling her." John's smile was warm on his son. "A woman is renting our hotel for five hundred dollars a month."

"What does she want with it?"

"It's the bar she wants. You can talk and be comfortable there."

"But there won't be any liquor, Pa."

"Oh, she knows that. She doesn't believe it. I felt bound to explain, because a man thinks a woman might not just be up on things, but she fixed me with those eyes of hers, and do you know, I think maybe she knows what she's talking about."

"But why our hotel?"

"There's local history there, and it's homey. But that's not the reason she's renting it."

"Then what reason?"

"Your mother did a small kindness for her, and some people don't forget a kindness. There must be hundreds of hotels in this state for rent. It was all—it was your mother's doing. Christ, how I do miss her."

"I miss her, Pa."

"There's a pair of us. How strange things turn out. Maybe Miss Talcott thought it lucky to rent the place. And we lucky for having hung on to it."

They ate supper of Van Camp's pork and beans, thick slices of bacon and cheese sandwiches fried in bacon fat. John brought up four bottles of Anheuser-Busch from the cellar. "Considering what's happened, let's eat in the dining room. We're not who we were yesterday."

Indeed I am not, Zack thought.

"Your mother liked candles on the table. I'll rustle up some. She said when you got older, candlelight was kinder. But she never needed candlelight."

They ate in candlelight. Zack spoke. "Pa?"

"What's on your mind?"

"Pa, how much money does it take, how much money does a fellow have to have for a girl to marry him?"

"I don't know why you're asking. That depends on the girl. Whether she wanted the fellow or what he had."

"Suppose she said once she wanted to be rich and famous."

"Well, I'd be troubled. First I'd think she wasn't a girl

you'd want. And then I'd think to myself, Well, why did she tell a man a thing like that when it would make him think she was after his money. Maybe she said it to make the man want to get rich and famous. Your mother never wanted anything. I was well fixed in those days, but she'd have married me if I hadn't a nickel—I think sometimes. Sometimes I wondered why she married me. I gave her emeralds because her eyes were green, like yours, but she wore them because it pleased me. Grubbing in the garden with those rings on. And she liked hats and she did have hats, but hats are a drop in the bucket. I liked traveling. She never cared for it, but she went along. They're gone now, the emeralds, all of them."

"There wouldn't be another girl like my mother."

"No. Of course not."

"But if there was a girl, and she just took the pit out of your stomach."

"Then I think if I had half of five hundred dollars a month, I would hightail it to her and I would say, 'Look here, this is the situation.' And she could say what she wanted. You wouldn't be the first man to be turned down, Zack. No man ever died of a nosebleed or a broken heart."

Chapter 15

For years, farmers and ranchers had allowed tin signs to be tacked to their fence posts after a dollar or two had changed hands. First were the ones that appealed to a man's craving for nicotine: HORSESHOE PLUG and BULL DURHAM. If a woman, passing in a buggy, noticed CLABBER GIRL BAKING POWDER or ARBUCKLE'S COFFEE, she might think, Well, if it's worth advertising, maybe it's worth a try.

When the new age dawned and wheels turned faster, RAVOLINE MOTOR OIL and KELLEY SPRINGFIELD TIRES came under the same deadly fire as the old rusting signs and were riddled with bullet holes—but no one ever heard a shot.

MOTORISTS WISE SIMONIZE.

That morning Zack was about to hose off the mud, wash the car and polish it.

But he left the car as it was. Rain from a sunny sky—the

mud was proof of the grandfather's prediction. If it compensated a little for being old, there was no harm in an old man's believing he had prescience. Zack pointed the Locomobile, mud and all, toward Salmon, Idaho.

Scarlet Indian paintbrush grew thick beside a creek on the Montana side of the mountain; he had never picked flowers before, but a gift of flowers might help explain his appearance. As he laid them on the backseat, they seemed a pretty poor excuse, a schoolboy's idea.

He drove up to the small brick house. It was she who opened the door. He could see she meant him to speak first.

"I thought I'd come back. I brought some flowers."

"I'm glad you did. Come back. Brought flowers."

She took the flowers; he followed her into the living room, a small room lined with books. He noted on the bottom shelf, where gravity determines such books should be placed, the dark green bulk of the *Britannica,* the edition his father had bought before their debacle. It contained the entire world's knowledge from the letter A as the first letter of the Phoenician alphabet to "zymotic," referring to certain diseases.

The grandfather rose from a Morris chair. "Good morning, sir. I expected to see you. Hear what you had to say about the rain." The old man smiled. "Or did you come to find out what she read? I saw you looking."

Anne was in the next room at the sink, arranging flowers.

"I didn't mean to be nosy, sir. I read a lot. My father reads a lot."

"You can tell quite a bit by what people read," the old man said.

On the shelf above the *Britannica,* Zack had noticed *The Scarlet Letter.*

"I'm afraid I'm curious."

Anne entered with the flowers.

Zack said, "I wish they were roses."

"I'm glad they're not. You picked these. My grandmother's favorite flower. What I remember of her—we waded in the creek looking for freshwater mussels. Once the Indians used them for wampum. I was six and she was older than the world at fifty. She was an Indian, you know."

"I know."

"Then why were you so wicked to Mr. Connard for speaking the truth?"

"Because he meant to shame you."

"But he didn't, you know."

"He didn't know that. When I was a kid, my friend was an Indian boy. We waded in the creek. He was a Tendoy."

After his words died, it seemed that everything in the room froze. The old man coughed.

Anne moved to the scarlet flowers and touched them. "My grandmother was a Tendoy."

Zack's lips parted. "I—"

She went on. "You look astonished."

"I was. For a minute. But it fits."

"Fits?"

"Like a puzzle."

The light was noon; the light immobile.

The old man said, "You two go to dinner at the Shenon House. It's easier for people to talk on neutral ground. You stay here, I'll have to go to my room, and you'll think I'm overhearing. I could go to the barn, but that's not the thing."

*

At a table apart in the Shenon House, she said, "I thought you'd come back."

"Why didn't you ask me to come in yesterday?"

"I wanted to think you wanted to come back more than I wanted you to come back. I didn't want to appear forward."

How easily they spoke. Was that a part of love? "A beautiful woman can't appear forward."

"Don't say I'm beautiful."

"Why not?"

"I've been told a thousand times. I don't believe in beauty, because it doesn't last. I'd rather you thought I was intelligent, or even interesting. Beauty has no use, except to attract, in the beginning. First the hands go, and then the lines come around the mouth and eyes, and then the sagging muscles, and then the reason many men think they love a woman is gone, and if he's decent, he's tied to her; if he isn't decent, he turns to a younger woman. Beauty and youth are traps to continue the race. Why the race should continue is another matter."

"I knew I'd come back," he said. "Why did you hope I'd come back? I'm nothing to look at. You know I've got next to nothing."

"As for your looks, I doubt you ever look into a mirror. I suspect you shave by feel. I wouldn't trust a man who counted on his image.

"You were protective. You didn't know I didn't need protection, but you were protective. Something weak in me responds to that. But chiefly I hoped you'd come back because—"

He was leaning forward on his elbows. "Because?"

"I knew you could be trusted; there's a place in the world for you. What is that place? What do you want to do?"

So this is what his father meant when he said women moved men to become rich and famous. "When I was a kid," he began, "I was fascinated by a magnet."

"By the unknown. By the possibilities of the unknown."

"In high school I duplicated every experiment of Marconi and Hertz. Radio waves."

"I've read a little."

"What I see, or what I saw, was a box like a phonograph on tables in cities where people don't know each other, and way, far away where there are no voices and no music."

"You're talking," she said, "about popular entertainment."

He stared across at her. "Why, that's exactly what it would be. Exactly."

"And there's nothing so popular as entertainment."

"I worked with a fellow in France. We both saw the big trouble with the idea. Noise. Static electricity."

"Of that, I understand only that you have to get rid of it. But you didn't?"

"One evening—one foggy evening—I heard a mouth harp as clear as music across water. And for a little while I hoped."

"What did you hope?"

"That I could make a circuit of some combination of vacuum tubes."

"To duplicate the conditions at that hour in that place. And so?"

"I saw the problem as next to impossible."

"But one evening for a few moments, the problem was solved. I think you can solve it again."

He shook his head. "A man might do such a thing, work a miracle, if somebody believed in him absolutely. If he was married to a girl like you."

She laid her knife and her fork beside each other on her plate. She looked directly into his green eyes. "So then, that is that." She reached across the table and touched his hand. "From the moment I saw you, I wanted to go to bed with you. I had to be careful about being forward."

*

When Zack got back from Salmon that night, his heart singing, he proceeded with a bizarre little rigamarole more characteristic of his father than of himself. In his room was a corner closet—a corner closet will sometimes strike an architect as a good thing to do with a corner, otherwise a corner has no purpose—and the door of the closet supported a heavy full-length mirror that had interested Zack only very, very briefly when he was just fifteen and suddenly every boy in high school was concerned with the style of his hair. A pompadour was the thing to have, a style perhaps suggested by a song popular a few years earlier.

Since the hair of very few grows naturally as a pompadour, tricks were devised to torture and train the hair to lie straight back as if that were meant to be. An unguent called Stacomb was on the market, but not popular with mothers, who complained that the stuff stained pillowcases and ruined the upholstery of any chair or sofa the treated head touched. Another trick was to wet the hair thoroughly, skin it back, and keep it in place by pulling over it, like a skullcap, the large end of a mother's or older sister's stocking.

Zack could not have brought himself to request a stocking from his mother for any purpose whatever, but as an almost desperate reader of encyclopedias, he understood that certain wild tribes in Asia boiled the seeds of the quince (held by some authorities to be the very apple in the Garden of Eden) and the result was a clear glue that would make of the hair whatever one wished.

Zack had long been on good terms with the old druggist, who for some years had been dispensing to Zack small vials of acids and packets of salts and bases and carbon tetrachloride for removing grease from electrical connections. The old druggist was all professional indifference to Zack's request for quince seeds, and Zack was not surprised that they were available since he knew that they had a medicinal as well as mucilage value.

Since Zack had a portable bunsen burner in his room, and both retorts and beakers, he need not trouble his mother about using her kitchen and her pots, and so could avoid questions she'd be bound to ask. "Quince seeds? Boiling quince seeds? And putting it in your hair? Is that what you mean to do?" Of all questions, a mother's are the most searching—and the most embarrassing because somehow one is so close to her.

And just as he had read, the seeds did yield a clear jelly, and it did seem to control his hair; but not for long. Nothing could, for long. His hair was given to determined partings that finished as cowlicks and spikes. It may well have been at that moment, when he realized that his hair could not be like the hair of everybody else, that he also realized that he himself could never be like anybody else.

There was absolutely nothing of vanity about him; he had early understood he had nothing to be vain about. He had never heard anyone say, within his hearing, "Isn't he a fine-looking boy." Nothing like that. Only, perhaps, "He has a nice smile," and "He has a quiet voice." And that always from older people.

But now suddenly, within the last four hours, he had been told by the loveliest woman in the world that she wished to go to bed with him. No, it was not vanity that made him stand nude before that full-length mirror in the corner. Not vanity, but wonder. He observed his naked body with a cold detachment and turned to get yet another view that might be more attractive to a woman. What on earth had she seen in him? But whatever it was, she had seen it, and she had chosen him above all others. Suddenly he grinned at himself, and then he sighed, but deep in his throat was a sob. Oh, but he did lie awake a long time that night, imagining so much and so much.

*

And so they were married, perhaps to choirs of angels, in St. Mark's Episcopal Church. St. Mark was represented in one of the Tiffany windows. He resembled a bearded old uncle and he frowned on the big book that rested on his left forearm—too large a volume to contain only the first three drafts of the Gospel according to him. It might have been the Old Testament he frowned on.

The centerpiece of one window was a young sheep that refuted all that is known about a true sheep's joints, for it carried aloft with its right hoof and foreleg the splendid banner of the Episcopal Church. Three pretty female saints whose names are lost in ecclesiastical history were almost hidden in luscious vines and pendant grapes. A similar confusion of vines climbed the vertical plumbing in the far corners of the dining room in the new Andrews Hotel across the street.

The light through these expensive windows tinted the little church with a small magnificence. It was out of the question, then, to speak; even so innocent a whisper as a request for a safety pin had the conspiratory tone of private prayer.

The oaken pews somewhat accommodated the human form, but the kneeling rails, pulled down when prayer was at hand, were cruel to the kneecaps.

Now stuffed with roses, the brass vases on the altar far up front gleamed from the handiwork of the Altar Guild. Lizzie had been a member; she was the churchgoer. It is noteworthy that many, many men assign religious duties to their wives or mothers, and should it turn out that there actually is a God, they might plead that they thought their women could handle it better. The Altar Guild was a select group in Grayling. To them it sometimes occurred, even when they were otherwise occupied—dancing, say, to the music of the Baxter-Tonrey Orchestra or to phonograph records, or playing bridge—to them it sometimes occurred in a moment of silence that they were indeed Christ's handmaidens. And so they were: they took seriously the white linen coifs they wore at work, and enjoyed being seen in them. And so gleamed the candlesticks, the one on the Gospel side and the one on the Epistle side, and so gleamed the big brass cross bearing at its interstice only the letters IHS. The Roman custom of showing Christ hanging from nails on the cross was thought excessively savage, if perhaps comprehensible for ethnic groups whose backgrounds had accustomed them to violent death.

The new young rector had himself been married but seven years. At the seminary at the University of the South, he had been instructed to counsel young people bent on marriage, and Zack and Anne were called into his little office in the rectory beside the church. Somewhere upstairs a baby whimpered. Zack and Anne sat opposite him; he made a tent of his thumbs and fingers and peered over it.

"Anne, my dear. Zack, dear son. So good of you to come. When I've finished, won't you stay for coffee? I don't have much to say, except that marriage is a holy estate, ordained by God. Do you believe this?"

"I'm ready to believe it," Anne said.

"Yes," Zack said.

"And you know it's not all going to be a bed of roses. Far from it. Not all pies and cakes."

What he was saying not very well is that two people about to get married haven't an inkling of what's ahead. Not an inkling. From his own seven years of marriage, the young rector had gained not much inkling.

There is, in marriage, the delight at being in the presence of the loved one, the sweet longing when the loved one is no more than a mile distant. There is the ecstasy of orgasm—of *jouir,* as the French put it, and nicely, too, since the word so resembles the verb *jouer.* There may be the pleasure of companionship, and sometimes a mystical bond between husband and wife that allows the one to know exactly what the other is thinking, a thought transference that makes them formidable partners at bridge.

There is also sickness and boredom and doubt. There is the hope of coming home at night to one thing and finding quite something else. There is the beautiful woman with the plain daughter, or the plain woman who is mother to the beauty. There is the successful father and the failed son, or the successful son and the failed father, the angry words, and then the drinking. Yes, and comes the time of the return home of the divorced daughter, the children who would have preferred to remain with the father, who have secrets they dare not tell, and then do tell them. Comes the return to the regulated household of the divorced son, and he without a job, critical and sullen because he'd been allowed to run wild as a child. Debt and foreclosure, the early death of the favored child who had always been known by the other children as the favored one.

Always a matter of money, of peculiar needs, and two young people who have lived next door all their lives—he who had heard her practice her scales on the piano for a dozen years and she who was long accustomed to the tentative roar of his motorcycle—these two come to realize they are entirely different human beings, almost a different species; lying awake at night they wonder what is to become of them, what the few remaining years will bring, and what is it all supposed to mean?

"And let me say," the young rector finished, "that I hope your life together will be the best that life can be." The reservation in those words was probably lost on all three of them. They all three stood. The young rector came to them and put his arms around both of them.

"May God be good to you."

Anne said, "I'm going to cry."

"Don't," the rector said. "Be happy. Now for some coffee."

A day later Anne Chapman walked up the red-carpeted aisle on the arm of her grandfather; his ancient suit was perfect for this ambience.

And Anne?

Hundreds of brides had walked up that red aisle with a father or a brother or a grandfather, and about each had been said, "Doesn't she make a lovely bride?" For no matter how plain or faulty the bride's features, no matter how badly fitted her bridal gown, at the moment when she is about to become the wife of a man, she is exactly what Nature intended, and something of that shows.

"Doesn't she make a lovely bride?" was not said of Anne Chapman, about to become Anne Metlen. Those words were entirely inadequate, and would seem almost a lie; for never before and probably never afterward did such a young woman walk on that red carpet.

It was the custom for a bride to wear something that her mother had worn at her own wedding—the veil, perhaps, or a crown of silk flowers or, best of all, her mother's entire wedding regalia, if she could get into it. Anne's mother's wedding had been so impromptu that Anne had no gentle past to bring to her costume. She wore, instead, Lizzie Metlen's wedding gown, and the thought crossed several minds (who knew what the situation was) that a great many men, in a very real sense, choose for their brides women very like their mothers. There may be more to the legend of Oedipus than meets the eye.

And it had been John Metlen's idea. He was enchanted with the girl about to be his daughter-in-law. When he first saw her, he had taken a step forward to touch her hand; she went to him at once and kissed him.

What could he do to make it clear to her what he thought of her? Ah! When she moved into the house, he would turn over his big room to her, where he and Lizzie had loved and laughed.

"It's too big a room for a man alone," he explained.

She had looked levelly at him, and then she smiled, he thought, in appreciation. "You will not move out of your room, or I will never move into this house. You are the Old Man here. It is you who has the experience."

Never before had he thought it a compliment to be called old, and never before had he thought of himself as experienced. "But I'd be happy to do so," he said.

"You must find some happiness elsewhere."

"Then," he said, and his voice broke a little. "Would you favor me by wearing Lizzie's wedding gown?"

"I should love to," Anne said. "I suspect I'm taller than your wife; isn't it providential that dresses are shorter now."

She walked in Lizzie's gown, a woman so different, a raven-haired Sphinx whose expression and words were open to interpretation. Walking in Lizzie's gown she commanded the little church and distracted the small congregation from the holy business at hand. Here and there was perhaps a little envy, even evidence of ill will, inexplicable except for her bearing that so set her apart she had no need of what others had to offer—themselves.

She left her grandfather at the altar rail, paused, and mounted to the altar, where Zack waited under the ninth Tiffany stained-glass window, a round one of Christ ascending into Heaven, His left foot placed to give Him purchase on a void that He might rise higher. That window had been the gift of old Martin Connard, whose son was not in attendance.

And so that night they went to bed, and oh, it was. Oh yes, yes, yes; it was, and to be.

She took a job selling clothes at Niblack's, called in advertisements in the *Examiner* "The Store Beautiful." The phrase was a strange choice of motto in a town where not much was thought of Latin tongues in which the adjective perversely follows the noun. Maybe Niblack had in mind the Paris houses of fashion. Niblack was a live wire and not born yesterday. Recently he had traveled to Chicago by Pullman car, at the rear of the train: he who truly valued his life and had the money for the extra fare rode there. Should the locomotive crash into something or leave the rails, those in the Pullman car might be no more than shaken up, cushioned as they were by the less fortunate up ahead.

He put himself up at the Palmer House and from there scouted Marshall Field's big store, where he noted a new trend. An entire department given over to powders, rouges, creams, lotions and perfumes was located near the entrance of the store so that the customer was welcomed by the fragrance of flowers and the odor of musk. Eastern women were giving themselves over to artifice, and the young women behind the counters were at least as fashionably dressed as the customers and, on the whole, as well spoken.

In the Store Beautiful he set up a similar if smaller section for the transformation of women, stocked it with the creations of Houbigant, Coty and Ciro; but his high card was placing Anne Metlen behind the counter. The Store Beautiful became a theater.

It was the tourist season; strangers came to fish the rivers and creeks and to pretend for a few weeks on the new "dude ranches." They drove into Grayling on Friday evenings, put themselves up at the new Andrews Hotel, rubbed elbows with cowboys in the Pheasant—and shopped at the Store Beautiful. They were enchanted, and Niblack knew it was not by the novelty of the perfume counter.

And how they must wonder that his employee arrived for work each morning in a Locomobile—no longer a new one by any means, but nevertheless a Locomobile.

But alas, good things do come to an end. Anne was almost immediately pregnant; after three months Zack and John raised such a fuss about her standing all day, and especially in such shoes, that she was bound to ask Niblack for time off until the baby was born, and then they would all see what they could do.

Niblack said, "Why, any number of women in town would be glad to care for a baby during the day. You'd be helping yourself and them, too."

And so a little boy was born in April when the country was fragrant with sagebrush and bright with lupine. Never had so many bluebirds been seen, nor had the meadowlarks sung so late in the evening. The birth was an easy one and took place at the hospital on the road out of town, where things were quieter.

It is hard to look at a newborn child and believe it can live in this alien world. And in spite of what new mothers and fathers and grandparents seem to believe, one baby looks very like another, and a sick baby differs little from a healthy one. The snares and pitfalls and disappointments so recently described by the young rector must eventually overtake Zack and Anne; they overtake everybody. But what happened almost immediately was at once simpler and far worse. The baby was born with a bone deficiency.

They hoped; there was a good deal of silence in the house, and they hoped.

"I'm ashamed I cried," Anne said. "I hate weakness in a wife."

Zack kept blinking. "The man can be wrong," he said. "A lot of times doctors are wrong. They're just human."

"I swear it will be all right. We will make it all right." She could see he was terrified, and she hugged him.

And so they sought other opinions. They carried the little child named John to Butte. Of Butte it was said, "A Mile

High and a Mile Deep." In Butte the doctors cared for the infirmities of the Copper Kings.

"I'm afraid we can do nothing." Doctors. Doctors . . .

"But have you heard of somewhere where something can be done?"

They had not heard.

So then it was Salt Lake City—the Crossroads of the West, the Western Chicago. The Crossroads of the West. Zack spoke the words like an incantation. There in Salt Lake were the Mormons, the Mormons so bent on health and well-being.

She and the little boy would go to Salt Lake City. Zack would remain behind and work on electrical circuits. They were a team. They worked for one end. For a little boy.

"I'll call you every night," she said, and so speaking felt their straitened circumstances, for a long-distance call was expensive. In those days the operator began by announcing, "Long distance is calling," and as when you received a telegram, your heart pounded; such expensive communications too often concerned death or other ultimate disasters.

The Union Pacific ran directly from Butte to Salt Lake City, a distance of five hundred miles; old John insisted that she take a compartment; old John would never get over his expensive tastes nor his conviction that anyone who belonged to him must be set comfortably apart. However, he said nothing about where she would stay in Salt Lake City. Perhaps he assumed it would be the Hotel Utah, where the crystal chandelier in the dining room was considered a wonder and lobsters packed in ice and seeweed were rushed to the kitchen from the state of Maine.

Anne found in Salt Lake City a clean, cheap hotel and made the little boy comfortable in a drawer from the bureau and a quilt from the foot of the bed. She called the hospital connected with the University of Utah; she explained her situation. The doctor with whom she spoke seemed kind. Surely there is bound to be a connection between kindness and professional ability. When she called Zack she spoke of the doctor's kind voice.

"Remember how I love you," Zack said.

And then he spoke for several minutes about an addition of ten feet he was making to the antenna in the little shack out of town, so he could reach additional ham operators by wireless telephone. All this to assure her that he was doing what he could to anticipate doctors' bills and traveling expenses.

Having given birth to a damaged child, Anne blamed herself; as another might believe that if she had not smoked, had eaten properly, had believed more in God, all would have been well, Anne blamed the Indian in her. She and Zack were genetically mismatched. Nature, in creating separate races, meant to separate. Who tampered with that ordinance did so at his own peril—Zack and she and her grandfather. But the horror was visited on a little boy now being tested in a Utah hospital.

Thinking of this, she bowed her head. Had she been Catholic she would have crossed herself.

"We'll see what we can do," the doctor had said. At the end of a week he called her at the cheap, clean hotel.

Oh, with what hope she left that spare and empty room. But she was not encouraged by the gentle kindness the nurse showed when she asked her to wait, just a few moments.

In the small waiting room there were toys so artfully distributed that they more resembled decorations than playthings, reminders that this was the outer office of a pediatrician and that some of the children who entered there might not live long enough to master the rocking horse.

The doctor came through a door in a business suit, wearing the sympathetic mien of the professional who assumes that we are all equally bereaved. There are physicians who hold out false hopes, just as there are parents who don't want to know. But some doctors speak the truth and let the chips fall where they may.

"I'm afraid," he said, "there is little hope, Mrs. Metlen."

Anne thought, Does not little hope mean there may be some hope?

He continued, "In the past years we have seen three such cases. Frankly, they are mysteries. From time to time these conditions do appear, but though someday they may be understood and conquered, we do not understand them yet. My experience with the others tells me only that you must not expect young John to live more than another five years." And before Anne could answer, he said, "You will of course want a second opinion."

A second opinion. Was that not what she and Zack had talked about? Even a third opinion?

In Salt Lake City there was another hospital, this one run by the Roman Catholics, known to the Mormons as Gentiles, since they are not of the true faith. But the Catholics supported a fine hospital and turned away no one who could pay the bills.

Anne carried the little boy by streetcar to Holy Cross. She looked and looked at him; he did not seem to her different from other babies, and if he had five years—by that time might not his condition be understood? She took it as a good sign that even though she had not called ahead, the little boy was taken at once to a ward where half a dozen other small ones lay, unknowing. Children and animals are fortunate to be ignorant of death.

She carried copies of tests and records made in the Butte hospital and in the Mormon hospital. Maybe materials from each, read and assembled at a third, could spell out hope.

The Director of Pediatrics was off in the mountains, fishing. However, the nurse had good news.

"He's expected back tomorrow. I've never known him not to get back when he's expected. Mrs. Metlen, he's an extremely dedicated physician. I may say also, a fine man."

Anne savored the word "physician," and the word "dedicated" verged on sanctity. A "fine man" would be gentle.

Meantime, she was appalled by the five dollars a day for

her room, by the hospital fees, even by the cost of food. In a secondhand store she bought a hot plate and smuggled it into the little hotel, feeling that the management might well object to a potential fire hazard and somewhat ashamed that finances had moved her to dishonesty. In an aluminum saucepan she heated up soups and pork and beans. She felt fortunate that she nursed the little boy.

When she called Zack long-distance, she spoke of the extremely dedicated physician, and how fine a man he was, according to someone who had no reason to say such a thing unless it was truly so. "He's to return tomorrow. He's the kind of man you can count on."

"I've ordered some new equipment." Zack's voice seemed to throb. "Nothing ventured, nothing gained." He would not have added that, she thought, unless it was very expensive equipment.

*

The Director of Pediatrics returned on schedule from a vacation in the Wasatch Mountains. Many returning from vacations are not anxious to assume harness at once but like to remain at home a day or so and savor the recent freedom. This man, though, went right back to work, and he called Anne.

Those who had funds sufficient only for such a hotel did not expect telephones in their rooms. A single telephone was in the hall on each floor; when it rang, somebody was bound to answer it—everybody hopes for a call. And he for whom the call was not walked the hall to alert the lucky person. It was kindness among strangers.

The telephone was just outside Anne's room.

"Mrs. Metlen, this is Dr. Bower. I've looked at your son's records."

"Yes?"

"I should like you to come and talk."

When she'd hung up, she stood for a few moments staring at the telephone.

*

Bower's office looked more like a formal living room than a doctor's office. Having passed like a stranger through the gates of Harvard Medical School because he was Boston Irish, and finding himself now beyond the pale among the spare and spartan Mormons, he chose to look about at Japanese prints and Chinese porcelains and to walk upon thick carpets, as questing in his tastes and intelligence and as exotic as a Jew. He was tall and thin, quite bald and gentle, and he inspired Anne's confidence.

"Please sit right down," he said, "and be comfortable. It would be unfair of me not to begin by saying there is nothing I can do for your son."

"Why have you asked me to come, then, doctor?"

"Because of a strange coincidence. We doctors are supposed to be up on the new things, the latest wrinkles. We go to meetings here and there, busy as beavers, and we read the medical journals. We are altogether curious about what others are doing in our profession. Sadly, in America we are behind the times. It may be because we did not have the casualties over here that offered such perfect—and dreadful—opportunities for French and German doctors to study both infection and disease and so to open up totally new fields in medicine."

"My husband was in that war."

"He came through unharmed?"

"Yes," she said. "He did." And she thought, And he came home to marry a woman who gave him a damaged child. Could Zack be said to have come home unharmed?

"I'd gone off on a little vacation, but before I left I gathered up some journals, promising myself I'd read them by lamplight. I think I knew all along I'd never glance at one of them. But the odd fact is, I did slit the cover of one journal. And read it. You can imagine my astonishment when I read your son's records to realize that not two days earlier I'd learned that work on his condition is going on right now in Paris and in Vienna."

"Then we must go to Paris or Vienna."

"I can give you the name of the two clinics." He hesitated, noting her slim bare fingers, her country clothes. Surely it is most cruel to offer hope that is beyond reach. But when God gives, man cannot meddle. So he said only, "It will be very costly."

She said nothing to this.

Help of a lesser sort, however, he could try to give. "I've had experience with handicapped children," the doctor said. "And with the parents. The child is not aware of his situation, and it is the mother, not the father, who suffers most. Please understand, so that you don't feel singular."

"My husband is not like that."

"He would not mean to be."

But it had in fact occurred to her that Zack might not love a damaged child.

"There is no way of knowing," he warned, "whether anything tangible can be done in either Paris or Vienna."

"But," she said, "there is hope."

Their eyes caught and held for a long moment.

She saw a kind but honest man.

He saw a brave but unsentimental woman.

So he sat down and took his pen and wrote, and then he rose and gave to her the reason for that hope.

*

As the train left Salt Lake City, the tracks ran close to the lake. A calm body of water should reflect the clouds that merge into quite recognizable shapes of England and France and the heads of monsters. But the flat salt water, unlike a mirror, did not reflect but absorbed images. The scraggly trees—cottonwoods, a few fruit trees—did not meet their inverted twins and were themselves, perhaps, but the reflections of imagination. How could they grow at all in that salt sand?

She had bought a bassinet; the little boy slept on the opposite seat. Some who could not afford the diner up ahead—

she among them—had opened box lunches, and the odor of hard-boiled eggs and orange peels crept through the car.

To her left was the lake and the straggling trees, and in her mind was a line from Byron. Childe Harold made a pilgrimage through Europe and observed the madness of war, the cruelty of bondage, the unchanging nature of human willfulness, man's indifference to experience, and he drank of the bitter but comforting cup of cynicism.

Anne moved her lips, her eyes upon the lake.

Like apples on the Dead Sea's shore, all ashes to the taste.

She had forgotten what Byron meant. Was it the futility of pilgrimage? Such as her own to Butte and then Salt Lake? But it was not the futility of pilgrimage that brought the line to her mind; it was the futility of pilgrimage without money.

Chapter
16

The earth trembled, the arm of the semaphore dropped, the train pulled into Grayling. Ahead, the engine paused and throbbed.

Anne stepped down with the little boy; Zack stepped up and hugged them both at once. They did not speak. They knew better than to speak. Speaking might disturb and topple very delicately balanced hopes. Since speech is human only, to speak must identify the three of them as human beings. Such is known far and wide.

*

Proof that Zack's circuit was perfected depended on human response—not on measurements and meters. He'd been in contact with a dozen ham operators for months; they would call him, or be silent.

Ham operators were seldom educated men, merely young fellows caught up in the excitement of radiotelephone in high school or in France. They were hewers of wood and drawers of water, garage mechanics, bricklayers, clerks in stores, sellers of Orange Crush. Instead of spending their youth and skill on motorcycles and shaving the heads of internal combustion engines, they sat night after night before their rigs, well into the black hours when the static was not so bad. Their headphones shut out the other world.

The married among them were not much understood, nor were they encouraged by their wives.

"You might as well be married to that thing. Far as I'm concerned, you are."

"Don't I hear you on the telephone with somebody all the time? You ought to listen to yourself."

"You never heard me talking on the telephone from the middle of the night till morning. You want to eat with me and the kids or fix up some kind of sandwich for yourself?" This might be at breakfast.

It was not ideas but facts that flew on the airwaves, facts about the weather, about a fire in a town, the possibility of an early winter, the intelligence of a man's dog. None of these young men had yet conceived of radio as home entertainment that would be as attractive to women as to men. It was perhaps their conviction (in those days) that women were a race apart that made them blind to the possibilities of what was right there before them. They clung to their role as operators/listeners. It never occurred to them that radio would so shrink the world that New York came clear to California.

But they did often speak to each other about the poor quality of radio reception, and how it varied. It seemed to Zack that if what they heard through their headsets was unusually clear, they'd get in touch with him.

To reach a greater number of them, he needed a taller antenna, and here was a nice coincidence: the old Metlen

Hotel had a tower. He already had the first seventy-five feet of the hundred he needed to reach a hundred more ham operators.

He wrote to Kaufman, who was "in the thick of things" back East. Through his father, who was a kind of doctor, Kaufman would be in touch with the scientific world, and through the scientific world with patent attorneys.

"If this thing," Zack wrote, "whatever it is, turns out all right *here*, I'll be dependent on you *there*. We'll figure a financial arrangement that's satisfactory to you. Say, I'll bet when we first shook hands we didn't either of us think we'd ever be talking financial arrangements."

He mailed the letter and hoped the gods and the fates would forgive his hubris.

From Kaufman he wanted an estimate of costs. How much patent attorneys charged. How to get a patent. How much to set up a broadcasting station, who must be called in to judge it for purchase or lease. What was such a patent worth?

All now depended (or so he thought) on his first broadcast from the Metlen tower to a scattering of ham operators.

To the puzzlement of Grayling, he and a couple of young fellows began to erect a scaffolding on the tower. Lucille welcomed the construction. Many came to her place, speculating, drinking. She had been correct in her opinion of the Eighteenth Amendment. Hudson Super Sixes—fast, tough cars—raced down from back roads left unpatrolled on the vast Canadian border. Lucille's was once closed for a week, but money changed hands. Everybody liked Lucille.

*

Zack carefully considered the nature of his first "broadcast" through his new circuit. He didn't want to announce over the air that something new in the quality of sound might be expected. He didn't want to influence by suggestion. Since the air was already filled with talk, Zack decided to broadcast music as an ear-catcher, and when the music had finished to speak a few words.

By 1917 almost everybody had a phonograph. Some called them graphophones, and some called them gramophones, but all agreed that the best one was the Edison. The Kimball was all right, and the Columbia was good, and the Sonora and the Victrola. Considering the superiority of the Edison, it might seem strange that "Victrola" and not "Edison" became the generic name for phonograph.

But the Edison was expensive; it did not use steel needles but a diamond stylus that seemed not to wear out; the tone arm moved exactly across the record, without distortion or error. The records were three times as thick as those of other makes, took up a great deal of space and were expensive to ship. An Edison phonograph, along with the Locomobile, was about the last expensive toy John Metlen bought before he failed.

It resembled an oaken coffin turned on end; the grille through which the music came was fretted with Gothic arches and backed by snuff-colored silk. In the drawer underneath was an odd collection of records; John's taste in music was certainly catholic. There was an arrangement with brass and winds of *The Pier Gynt Suite*. "In the Hall of the Mountain King" was played most often because of the nice crash at the end of it. *The Egyptian Ballet* sounded so Egyptian it was surprising that an Italian had composed it; one could well imagine a frozen frieze of maidens, shoulders and breasts to the front, heads in profile, and suddenly reviving the past. There were operettas, "Gems from *The Runaway Girl*," "Gems from *The Red Mill*" and more of Victor Herbert. Since both Caruso and Amelia Galli-Curci were under contract to Victor, John bought an attachment for his Edison, and he and Lizzie enjoyed *I Pagliacci* and "The Bell Song."

Zack thought first of broadcasting Sousa—"Stars and Stripes Forever" or "The Washington Post March"—but he considered the age and taste of the ham operators, and decided on a popular song called "Jada."

The song was empty and it was catchy; except that we now hear almost nothing of robins and rivers and bluebirds and much more of social complaint, popular songs have not much changed.

Zack and John moved the Edison in the Locomobile to the hotel and set it up in the tiny room below the tower; already Zack had relocated his ham rig there, and his headset. He intended to be listening to the air immediately after his "broadcast." In the meantime, his handmade microphone was ready behind the silk grille of his phonograph. Lucille and her customers were interested.

Zack wanted no strangers around when "Jada" was put on the air—just why, it would be hard to say. Maybe to him the experiment cried out for the same privacy as sex. He decided on a midnight, just after Lucille had said goodbye to her last customer, midnight when the air was kindest to radio, and the dedicated hams were all in their places, headphones clamped on tight.

Only Zack and Anne were present at what might become something or other. John remained at home with the baby. "I diapered Zack a thousand times, and never once stuck him with a pin." It was clear to him that the little boy of almost three months loved him. The child smiled at him, quite unaware of a possibly brief future. Like animals, children are lucky in not knowing of Death; not until they bury a dead bird in a matchbox with great pomp and pagan honors do they sense that oblivion sits just out there. But this little smiling boy might never live to bury a bird, an idea his family rejected out of hand.

"The boy's mine tonight," John said.

Anne and Zack left the house under a new moon.

In the tiny room at the bottom of the steep, narrow stairs up into the tower, it was quiet. No electric light had ever been installed there, and the power lines that fed the transmitter at the top of the tower snaked in under the door from the lobby. Zack had a flashlight. Anne scarcely breathed. Maybe they prayed; certainly prayer was invented as a last resort by men to achieve what they already have viewed as improbable. To what they prayed, if they prayed, neither one of them could have said, but if they prayed it was certainly to some principle of fairness. Why should a little boy not have a chance to live?

Into the tiny room from the rooms above there came filtered creakings of the night. The courthouse clock struck midnight.

Zack whispered, "All right. Here we go."

"Wait!" She went to him and buried her head in his chest. Into his chest she spoke. "Whatever happens is all right. Whatever happens. Remember." She kissed him. "Now," she said.

Zack turned the flashlight on an H switch. He threw the switch. From above came a faint humming, as of distant bees. He turned the light on the phonograph, lifted the lid. He dropped the record "Jada" on the turntable; he cranked the machine. The turntable moved. He raised and positioned and lowered the diamond stylus. He closed the lid. The music began, dainty with fiddles, picky with banjo, perky with drum. Then came a high, hysterical man's voice singing.

The record lasted but four minutes. Then Zack removed the microphone from behind the grille and spoke into it. "This is Zack Metlen, W2XW in Grayling, Montana. I was in the war, too. I hope it seems like a long time ago."

He sat before his rig, and clamped on his headphones. He had almost no hearing in his right ear. He had been scared quite a few times in France. One shell had exploded too close for the right ear.

Scared quite a few times. How he hated death. And when things were quiet, he thought again and again of how precious a man's life was, and only on loan to him. Turning in upon himself, and in another man's country, he'd sort over the years and days, searching for what it was that made his own life precious, what it was he wanted, what he remembered, and time and again what stuck in his mind was a sound as ephemeral as life itself, and so tangible he might have held it in his hand. What lay in his mind was the striking of the courthouse clock for the dark hours, the single stroke for half past midnight, for one, and for half past one. To himself and to no one else, he spoke of those single strokes as the Three Ones, and they had been intimate companions his third year in high school when in those dark little hours he balanced equations concerning the speed of light and the nature of sound.

It did not at all surprise him, now, that shortly after the single stroke for half past midnight, he heard himself called.

"Calling Metlen. W2XW."

Zack spoke. "W2XW."

"I think you started something, buddy. And it goes Jada."

Anne went home. Zack was up the rest of the night. She brought him coffee and they drank it as the sun came up.

*

The letter Kaufman wrote from Boston was disturbing in several ways. Kaufman believed him to be the son of a rich man; Kaufman could not have expected him to be dumbfounded at a sum of twenty-five thousand dollars "to get it all together."

He wrote in detail.

There's an abandoned shoe factory twenty miles west of Boston with a tall water tower, for an antenna. There's a board of selectmen in town and what you do along that line is get a "permit to operate." I laughed when I tried to explain to one of the selectmen what you wanted to do. You'd pay the town about two hundred dollars for your permit.

Equipment doesn't come cheap, and if you want to reach way out, you're going to have a fair-sized generator. And patent lawyers don't come cheap because they know how anxious a fellow is to get a patent.

But you can handle all of that. Twenty-five thousand would be a fortune to me, old sport.

Twenty-five thousand dollars.

"But," Kaufman wrote,

• 201 •

.ike the fellow says, time is of the essence. You and I both know that a funny thing hangs around any invention. There's another fellow breathing right down your neck. It was that way about the typewriter, and even now over in France they think they invented the phonograph and have papers to prove it. Who invented the automobile? I guess the reason somebody's breathing down your neck is that everybody's reading everybody else's research, or maybe it's what they call the Zeitgeist. It says in the Bible there's a time for everything, and you've got to be the first for this everything and get the patent.

Come on back here and let's get started. There have to be a lot of tests, and a lot of arguing, because those with the money want a sure thing. But I always figured you for a winner. Bet your wife's pretty. You deserve a pretty one because you're a good guy. A woman can be a big help to a man. That's what it's all about, isn't it?

Twenty-five thousand dollars.

Zack had believed a few thousand at the outside, and he had believed that even that would be put up or advanced by any "interested party."

It was absurd to consider asking Connard for a loan; even if the fellow believed in the project, he'd refuse Zack Metlen. Connard didn't need another fortune.

Zack drove north to Butte, city of the Copper Kings, city of the Metals Bank, founded by W. A. Clark himself, who died leaving seventy-five million dollars and a castle in New York City.

"Metlen," the man said there, musing. "I remember your father, John Metlen." The man spoke as if John were dead. He and Zack spoke in a private room. When Zack talked of his scheme, he might as well have suggested going to the moon. "You see what it is," Zack said. "It's popular entertainment."

Bankers in those days did not like the word "entertainment." Entertainment is ephemeral; people interested in entertainment are not much to be trusted. You have only to look about you. That the public might want a box in the house for entertainment that came through the air . . .

Another bank. Same thing.

Zack drove back to Grayling.

They held a family conference—a fine idea. A decision formulated by several has greater thrust.

The family conference ended on something like euphoria. For Anne, the euphoria may have been tinged with hysteria. The little boy was not gaining weight. She had hoped that had nothing to do with bone deficiency but was something that might afflict any little child.

The local doctor thought that not the case. She said nothing of this to Zack. The little boy continued to smile, trusting in life. She would stand above him. "You will live. I promise."

She had once been indulgent of her grandfather's belief that he had powers of divination, but life itself is so strange, cannot its strangeness include strange powers? The legends say so. Wasn't it possible a daughter had inherited a grandfather's powers? To see the future, a child grown well and strong because of a mother's sheer will? Hers was an unreasonable and towering state of mind, but suppose she were able to exchange something more than her own death that the little boy might live and be well? Dying for a child would be nothing.

The family conference decided that Zack should travel by train to Chicago. Why had they not thought of Chicago before? Second-largest city in the land, forward-looking, rose like the phoenix from a great fire, land of the Potter Palmers, the Marshall Fields. There it was that Cyrus McCormick had lived, and no doubt some foolish banker in Butte or Salt Lake City had turned him down flat, when he came, hat in hand, with plans for his reaper. Chicago! There you'd find a banker with guts and imagination. Was twenty-five thousand so large a sum to Chicago?

His father, wife and son saw Zack off on the train—made

a little party of it, and as the train pulled away they waved until it snaked around the first curve. To wave and wave and wave and wave until that train was out of sight was necessary.

*

And so it was that Zachary Metlen was not on hand for the thirtieth anniversary celebration of the founding of the town of Grayling, Montana.

Preparations had gone on for months. Indians had been hired from the reservation in southern Idaho to dress up in buckskin, put on their war bonnets, and "attack" a troop of white settlers lounging around three covered wagons. It is not easy to reconstruct a covered wagon, and no thought was given to the fact that in 1880, when Grayling might be said to have been founded, covered wagons were long past, making the show on the fairgrounds an anachronism. But Indians and covered wagons would certainly establish the fact of the Past. As for the Indians, whose transportation was to be paid for by the city of Grayling, they had to reconstruct war bonnets and bows and arrows. Their own, the real ones, they had long since sold to tourists and to the state museum.

The big attraction would be the rodeo. Strings were pulled, and the American Rodeo Association announced that the Grayling rodeo would be of championship stature; the best bronc riders, calf ropers, bull riders and clowns in all the West would be on hand. The *Grayling Examiner* revealed that several lady bronc riders would appear, with names like Bonnie, La Verne and Arlene. These women lived wildly incomprehensible lives with men often not their husbands, in tents and boardinghouses. They smoked cigarettes, they drank, they behaved like the show people they were, aware of the brevity of life.

The celebration at the fairgrounds would conclude with the stagecoach race. Stagecoaches had been solicited from a dozen cities in Montana; these cities, having so little past and proud of what there was, kept a stagecoach on display as a tourist attraction. How suddenly and inevitably does a means of transportation become passé; already it is common to see a steam locomotive, lonely but still potentially powerful, on a single length of track in a public park where children come, and fathers attempt to explain.

The Grayling celebration was to last all one Friday and all one Saturday in mid-June of 1920. Some talked of extending it through Sunday, but a plethora of Baptists and other fundamentalist taxpayers objected to hilarious and abandoned activities on the Sabbath.

Even as Zack left for Chicago, a rough element had begun setting up booths covered with canvas in case of rain where vendors would sell weenies (the word "frankfurters" was unknown) and hamburgers and Orange Crush. At some booths, a man might throw baseballs at a row of wooden ducks that traveled on a canvas belt before a backdrop painted to resemble water. Should he strike and upend a duck, he might win what from a distance appeared to be an Indian blanket; if a girl was with him, he might choose the kewpie doll.

Even as Zack left, the chutes were prepared to keep the bucking horses still so a man could let himself onto their backs. Before Zack arrived in Fargo, North Dakota, the air over the fairgrounds was heavy with dust and new manure and frying fat. The high school band looked to their uniforms, and the bandmaster, L. A. Gregory, put them through a final practice in the high school gymnasium, a cavernous space still festooned with blue and yellow crepe paper from the Junior Prom.

What lent this celebration a particular cachet would be the appearance in town of important people from a distance. The mayors of both Great Falls and Missoula would sit in the grandstands, along with the president of the university. Several Copper Kings from Butte had agreed to come. But the biggest plum was the governor of the state. Bigger plums might have been Montana's senators, but they, alas, were tied up in Congress over war reparations and the Dawes Plan; it was comfortable knowing that two such dedicated and astute men represented Montana in such complicated matters, one bushy-browed and white-maned, the other thin, frowning and dogged. Before long these two fine men would so embarrass the Harding Administration with cruel questions that heads would fall.

But a governor is a governor, and likely to become a senator himself one day. His lady had stunning presence and moved in worldly circles. They could appear only for the Saturday celebration, and that evening would grace the head table in the dining room of the Andrews Hotel for dinner and dancing to the Baxter-Tonrey Orchestra.

The gathering in the dining room of the Andrews Hotel would make clear who counted in Grayling. There was not space for everybody, hardly room enough for the early settlers, their children and their in-laws and a couple sneaked in because they had amassed money. The Metlens had received an invitation. Although the Metlens had lost everything, the Metlens were still the Metlens; to refuse them an invitation was to make a cruel but dangerous statement about money, a statement no local noble dared make. He himself might be strapped one day, and barred from some door.

The Metlens did not answer their invitation. About this, there was dissatisfaction in many quarters. A shame that Lizzie was not still alive to appear that evening with John. For years they had suspected some explosive confrontation between Lizzie and old Connard; too bad he and Lizzie weren't still alive, that they might come face to face. At socials, she had been excessively polite to him, but smiling a smile that scorned. Like a disease, the enmity had been passed on down.

For there had been a ruckus in Salmon, Idaho, and young Connard had lain sprawled in the dirt. Zack Metlen's wife had to do with it, and her appearance would have given satisfaction on several counts. She was as much a showpiece, as much a tourist attraction, as any restored stagecoach, any spectacular waterfall, any cleft in the earth or lofty structure. And what a play of emotions might have been seen—young Connard present, Zachary Metlen and his wife present, and the governor's queenly lady. Anything might have happened, and for what reason does anybody go anywhere except that anything may happen?

In the rodeo on Friday, a bronc rider from Montana had clearly outshone riders from Idaho, Colorado, Wyoming and North Dakota. To start things, a parade of men and women rode horses around the outer limits of the fairgrounds. Like the horses themselves, some of the riders were fading into the past, and for this occasion they borrowed horses and so became for a day a part of the cowboy-Western mystique, perhaps the only true American folk culture—careless, colorful, tragic and maybe brave—and the source of great profit for the moving pictures. Leading the parade was Grayling's mayor; with difficulty he managed the reins and the American flag at the same time. Dozens of riders followed in cowboy boots and big Stetsons. Some among the women wore fringed leather divided skirts like Annie Oakley's, and some dared to wear men's Levi's, let out and altered and pieced at great pains to fit the female hips and rump. The necessary but unpleasant defecation of the horses marred the scene in the eyes of the fastidious, and the parade was a bit disorderly when a horse stopped dead in its tracks to urinate while the rider tried to look unconcernedly into the distance. A peculiar entry in the parade was a new Stutz touring car, far beyond the reach of those in the bleachers; it proceeded on but three wheels, slyly hinting that all was possible.

Most memorable that Friday afternoon, the sun high and hot, glancing off the brass of the trombones and the tubas of the band—most memorable was the goring of a clown by a Brahma bull that had tossed its rider. It was the duty of clowns to divert the bull's attention from a rider it had tossed, and the clowns were made up exactly as in circuses, the bulbous noses, arched eyebrows, gashlike mouths and funny pointed hats. They were usually as skillful as bullfighters at dodging sharp horns. An ambulance rushed in at once through a gate beside the bronc chutes; such a conclusion had been contemplated. Whether or not the clown died was not known for some time, for immediately the bronc riding began and that Montana boy outrode all the rest.

The clown died up at the hospital even before the nurse could remove his makeup. But that man had deliberately chosen a dangerous vocation; when you do that, you've got to be prepared to pay for the dazzling, carefree life you chose. Men who walk on steel girders on skyscrapers know this.

The stagecoach race on Saturday raised a good deal of dust; the sun remained high and hot. The governor's lady, who sat apart with other celebrities in a loge draped in red-white-and-blue bunting, was seen to press a handkerchief to her face; there was much coughing; she was glad, that afternoon, to get back to the corner room in the Andrews Hotel and into something cool and loose. She and the governor ordered up a carafe of ice water and a bucket of ice. The governor removed a bottle from his grip and mixed some of the contents with ice in a hotel glass.

"I'm ready for a drink," he said. "You want one now?"

"How long have we got before dinner? Don't want some local teetotaler smelling it on my breath. You men have all the best of it. You are accountable to nobody. Your only problem is that you've got to shave."

He removed his watch. "We've got two hours."

"Then by all means."

Downtown the bars were crowded; it was impossible to get inside Lucille's. Lucille nodded and smiled among her customers and played the great lady. The whores in the Red-White-and-Blue Rooms were bathing their parts and arranging their hair into attractive shapes. It's next to impossible to curl hair without burning some; the smell of burning hair sets your teeth on edge—especially when you begin to think of things.

But up the street, near the hospital where the clown was dying, the sidewalks were deserted. In the living room of the silent Metlen house, John sat at a table playing solitaire.

Ever since Adam, men's lives have been in disarray; and men seeking order and meaning have invented gods, and prayed to them; have wished on stars, noted the flight of birds, and examined the entrails of sacrificial beasts. Men interpret dreams, note the lay of tea leaves—and lay out cards.

Of the cards John had asked a question, and asking it, he wondered if he was worthy to ask it. It was the ultimate question—one to be asked, probably, by one who had suffered a good deal more than he had. As for him, he had no more than lost his worldly possessions, lost his wife to a choking disease, and despaired of the life of his grandson—a paltry list of woes compared to other lists. But he had gone ahead and asked the cards, Is there any reason to hope?

Not for himself (he told himself) had he asked, but for the others, for the next generation. For him, time had about run out, and soon another little procession would form at the foot of the hill. But selfishly, he had, deep down, asked for himself as well, and he laid out the cards: if he won the game, he might hope, have reason to hope. If he did not win the game—well, that was the chance a gambler took, and the failure at so preposterous a gamble was on his head. A man doesn't get to ask that question twice. If the answer is no, a man must live with that, as many live with that. The first card, he remembered, was the four of diamonds.

The telephone rang. His heart paused.

The telephone had first rung in that house twenty years before. It was John who had decided they needed a telephone, and he who had stopped in to see the telephone company, he who watched the man climb a pole with iron claws strapped to his feet, who watched the stringing of the wires and the phone screwed to the wall in the hall. But when it rang for the first time, his heart paused.

It paused now, and his mouth went dry. Carefully he laid down the deck of cards, but before he could rise from the table—his legs wouldn't work—he heard Anne on the stairs. She hurried to the telephone, and as she passed him, they exchanged fleeting smiles. Oh, so much pretense. Does not the skull appear to smile?

He heard her say, "Zack." And because the telephone was in the hall, he couldn't watch her face. For some moments she said nothing. Then, "We'll expect you on Tuesday's train."

That meant Zack was leaving Chicago within the hour. But what was in Anne's voice? It was strange about her—when she spoke you might get two different meanings. Two people heard different things, just as these cards before him could tell one man one thing and another man another.

His knees let him stand. When Anne came from the telephone, she paused and stood absolutely still before him. Now, stillness is stillness, is it not? But her stillness was another matter—a stillness with infinite dimension, in which all was possible—but she herself unreachable except to Zack Metlen. Why only him? Zack was a good young man but no better looking than his father, and that was saying but little. John had often wondered at his luck with Lizzie, often thought she'd have been as happy with many another man; she had a gift for making do. But Anne would have only Zack. He had been chosen. Set apart. Had she some vision of him, clear to her but dark to others? Why had these two taken each other?

She spoke. "He can't get the money."

So that, then, was the answer to his question, and he'd not yet even laid out all the cards. He was about to speak a platitude, about to smile, and to say, "Well, it's not the end of the world."

But for one of them perhaps it was.

He couldn't speak. It was she who did. "I'm going up now, to dress. I'm going to dinner at the Andrews Hotel."

She walked past him, and up, and he understood Job 4:15.
Then a spirit passed before my face; the hair of my flesh stood up.

Chapter
17

In that year when fashion demanded yards of cloth arranged in swags, braid, tassels, fringe, feathers and monkey fur, the dress Anne wore, bought at the Store Beautiful at a salesperson's discount, was strikingly simple, a black velvet sheath; it may have been sent out from New York by mistake. In Grayling, women dressed in black only to visit the dead, or to sit in a darkened room where, in a room apart, someone lay dying. Except for a silk cord around the waist, which she immediately discarded, the dress—frock, they said then—was entirely without ornamentation, and called attention entirely to herself. She had never before worn it.

She sat in it before her dressing table—Lizzie's dressing table—and saw herself in the three mirrors. Below, in a drawer, was what remained of Lizzie's jewelry, nothing there of value. All had been sold to save the ranch; what remained would today be called costume jewelry, but "casual pieces" then—bits of turquoise set in silver, coral earrings carved into roses, an oval brooch of glass covering a lock of human hair. Anne had never had jewelry, nor had she ever wished it. It is likely now that she wanted to wear something of Zack's mother's, maybe for good luck. At her hand was a choker of false pearls; they were of good color and underscored the shocking simplicity of the black velvet frock.

Before the three mirrors she piled her black hair high. She rose.

She tucked the Metlen invitation into her black-beaded clutch purse, threw a cape over her shoulders and walked downstairs.

She said, "Young John's asleep."

John said, "If he wakes up, I know just what to do."

She put her hand on his shoulder. "Yes, you do," she said. But so did she.

She stepped out of the house and walked toward the carriage house; it was that hour when poppies fold their petals against the dark.

*

In the dining room of the Andrews hotel, everybody was about to sit down. Anne handed her invitation to a waiter stationed beside the curtained glass doors to refuse entry to the unasked.

"Evening, Mrs. Metlen," he said. "Zack away?"

"Back East," she said.

There was, as always when she entered a room, a short silence. Anne walked directly to the governor and his lady.

"It is good of you to come down for the celebration," she said.

The governor was affable. "Not at all. My wife says I'm territorial as a wolf."

"As a coyote," his lady said. "Mrs. Metlen, I'm very pleased to meet you."

She seemed to mean this, and she probably did. A woman

of great presence and normal curiosity, she had certainly heard about Anne Metlen.

And she had nothing to fear from Anne and was not in awe of her: they were two powerful women. The older, because she was the governor's lady and perhaps had a little hand in governing herself, if only from time to time when her husband did not feel himself. The younger, simply because she was.

Beside the swinging doors into the kitchen regions hung a set of mellow chimes. They sounded. The governor seated his lady; other men seated theirs. As Anne had hoped—and took as a good sign—she was placed not quite exactly opposite Harry Connard. The waiters began to hover. Harry Connard caught her eye, and she gave him a faint smile.

There had been doubt during the plans for the celebration about wine at dinner. Prohibition was now the law of the land, and the governor was bound to observe it. But had he always? No, he had not. He was known to have had drinks, and real ones, with dozens of men who sat now in this room. But that had not been in public. The newspapers were not likely to print the names of those seen drinking at Tina's Place outside of Butte, or a hundred other roadhouses. Those who reported for the newspapers were likely to be drinking in those places, not investigating. Everybody knows what newspapermen are, and why. They've simply seen too much.

However, some who had been invited into the dining room had been opposed to alcohol long before Prohibition, apparently for religious reasons, based on what in the Bible nobody knew. It is true that in the Old Testament, man is, from time to time, urged to be "sober," but that might mean to be serious and not always thinking about having a good time, meeting new women, playing cards, drinking, joyriding, things like that.

But was not the governor somehow above a law meant to prevent people from doing what they were going to do anyway? He and his lady frequented charmed circles as far as the East Coast, where gin and whiskey were the rule.

So wine was served. It was served from pitchers and came down from Butte in bulk, brewed there by the big Italian population. It was called Dago Red. It was not good, but it was festive and had a kick, and the governor need not leave town under the impression that Grayling was a nest of prigs. What would happen after dinner, everybody knew. There was hardly a car parked out front where a bottle couldn't be found, far stronger than Dago Red, and when the dancing began, you could bet it would be found.

If the governor's lady was aware of the impropriety of serving red wine with roast chicken, she made no issue and allowed her glass to be filled. To her left sat the mayor of Grayling, owner of Grayling Feed and Seed; he was tall and gray and stooped. In his earlier days as simply an employee of Feed and Seed, he had half killed himself lifting sacks to prove himself worth his hire. It was his understanding of what a man suffers that made him reluctant to press his customers for money. Most of them paid. Those who didn't, could not.

When everybody was seated and the wine poured, he stood, honored and respected and three times elected to represent the town, and he proposed a toast. All toasts are an embarrassment, like singing "Happy Birthday."

"A toast," he said, and they rose. "Here's to the city of Grayling," he said, and took a sip of wine. Others did likewise. "We are a small city, but we have big hearts." There were few hearts like his, and they gave him a fine ovation. Speaking is not easy before people, some of whom are strangers.

Waiters came with pitchers and refilled glasses; the governor's lady was seen to hold her palm just above her glass to indicate "enough." It is not to everyone's advantage to be considered a good sport; some must hold themselves apart, that others might attempt the same. It was not noted that Anne refused the first glass and the second. Her need was deep and not to be assuaged by Dago Red.

It takes little time to eat up sliced hens' breasts, pale gravy over mashed potatoes tortured by an ice-cream scoop, pale peas that had absorbed the taste of tin, and cranberry sauce. This homely, scarlet condiment—egregious in the month of June—evoked in some a recollection of disappointing holidays. Was there one single Christmas as perfect as was hoped? When there was not disappointment, and things thought if not said?

The small talk that was talked from left to right was the kind of banter that interested Zachary Metlen. The men spoke across their wives of the lack of wind around Grayling; many country people who lived far from streams were dependent on windmills for water. Women spoke across their husbands of the High Cost of Living in spite of what they understood to be the recent depression. The phrase "Butterick pattern" was spoken, and the astonishing change in the hemline noted.

"Well, I don't know," a man was heard to say in a way that meant he did indeed know. "Well, I don't know, but this man Harding looks the man to nominate. He sure looks like a President."

That man was young Harry Connard. As a banker, he was expected to know what he was talking about; politics and banking go hand in hand, and if you don't know about politics you can't be much of a banker. "He did great things for Ohio."

A stranger from Butte appeared to agree with him. "Well, the man paved all the roads in Ohio with bricks. I'll say that for him."

"Yes, he did," Harry Connard said.

"And Warren G. Harding," the stranger said, "got a kickback on every brick that was laid."

We are told and told not to discuss politics or religion or sexual preference with anyone with whom we hope to remain friends. The stranger might as well have announced that he could not take seriously anybody who was not an Episcopalian. A silence fell over the gathering. If what the

stranger said was true, then Harry Connard was condoning
a dishonest man. If Harry Connard did not know that Warren G. Harding had profited from bricks, then he did not
have the information he should have had.

Harry Connard fell silent, and his silence attracted eyes.
When an extremely handsome man falls silent, he falls extremely silent. There is a great power in a good-looking man,
or there seems to be, as was later borne out by Warren G.
Harding himself.

Nobody likes trouble, and it was a relief when the unfin-
ished Neapolitan ice cream began to melt and the Baxter-
Tonrey Orchestra arrived with their instruments in black
leather cases. The upright Kimball piano was already there.
The necessary moving and removing of tables and the broadcasting of wax granules across the hardwood floor to make
dancing easier smoothed over the recent altercation. The
Baxter-Tonrey Orchestra were five. Mrs. Baxter played the
piano; she was hanging on to her youth, but had to peer
closely at the sheet music. All five, including Mrs. Baxter,
wore light blue blazers with brass buttons. Mrs. Baxter alone
did not sport a clean white pocket handkerchief sharply
folded in the breast pocket. Handkerchiefs in breast pockets
are reserved for men; but embroidered in gold on her
pocket, as on theirs, were the letters B/T. It's a nice little
thing to have a monogram.

In those days it was accepted that the chief use—if not
the only use, alas—of the pocket handkerchief was for
blowing your nose. It was not thought a filthy habit to then
tuck the handkerchief back into the pocket and use it again.
But a creeping understanding of hygiene caused the appearance of Kleenex, which is, God knows, everywhere—
wadded up under beds, fluttering from low bushes, caught
in the branches of tall trees. But a handkerchief was also a
decoration, and a signal that one would not be caught un-
prepared.

Mrs. Baxter sounded an A on the Kimball; her husband
matched it on his fiddle, and tuned up. Tonrey removed

from its case his five-string banjo. Out came the saxophone, and the drum from its canvas case.

As the orchestra prepared itself, there were goings and comings; bottles appeared, some of them containing pink or green or orange sweet liquids; these, mixed with alcohol, were offered to those ladies who felt easier about drinking what was prettily colored—Orange Blossoms, Pink Ladies, fizzes of Crème de Menthe.

The Baxter-Tonrey Orchestra struck up "Dardanella," and then "Hello, Frisco" as appealing to the older folks. Quite a few of the older folks had already left. It was already around nine, and there was the pan to be removed at home from under the icebox. Some older people didn't understand the new music, nor much approve it. They had loved and understood the square dance but had not taken to the waltz, and as for the fox-trot, even the young people looked silly doing that, while the old were plain pathetic acting young. Though you had to hand it to Mrs. Tonrey for trying.

Among those who left were the governor and his lady; they were followed out to the white-tiled lobby by some well-wishers who had not been drinking much.

"But things are just getting going, governor," the undertaker said. However, as a politician in a state with conservative pockets, the governor knew that when things got going, it was best to be gone himself. Their chauffeur followed them into the dark street before the Andrews Hotel.

One and all could see that the governor was not drunk. The sobriety of those to whom he now showed a clean pair of heels was not so easily established.

"I want you to lend me some money," Anne Metlen said to Harry Connard.

You never knew just how drunk Harry Connard was; that was one of the great things about him. He had asked Anne to dance with him. Everyone near them had heard him, and then near and far, everyone saw them dancing, and they said to themselves, Well, bad feelings can't go on forever. In this brief life, everybody has to come to terms.

Every third dance was a waltz—the waltz from *The Merry Widow*, "The Gold and Silver Waltz," such things. The dancers expected to be dancing until midnight or later. It is not without pride that a woman will say, "We danced until three." She means, "That's how in love we were."

When Anne Metlen spoke of the loan she wanted, it was just ten-thirty. The courthouse clock had struck the half hour, and it was far too early to cease merriment. The children at home were all right. A mother was there, or a grandmother happy to be with the children.

Then suddenly the evening took a strange and ugly turn, something to remember for the rest of their lives.

"What is it you best remember?" you ask.

"The first time I saw my wife," you hear.

"The first time I saw my husband," you hear.

To answer otherwise is disloyal. It may even be the truth. But many people can't be at all candid about memory. They cannot admit atrocious acts, which they take to be singular. Memories should not be made of such stuff.

And so you hear a scene from childhood, when life was forever, and shimmered in light. "My first bicycle."

A woman smiles. "When I had my ears pierced." The piercing of the ears made a woman a woman as surely as the piercing of her hymen. An earring thrust through a hole in the earlobe and secured by a stout little nut is not so likely to fall into the crevasse in the cushions of a sofa; a woman with pierced ears might look forward to wearing true pearls and flawless diamonds with some safety.

"I need to borrow money."

Money is not to be spoken of in public. Your own bank balance will not be revealed to you over the telephone unless the bank teller recognizes your voice, and you make a telling remark that assures him that he knows you. The money you have or have not is a measure of exactly how most people will use you. Money will open most, if not all, doors. It is the single commodity that will get you almost anything.

In asking for money, Anne Metlen might as well have

spoken in public of sex, seldom mentioned because of the trouble it causes.

"Your husband wasn't man enough," Harry Connard said, "to ask for it himself? For that crazy scheme of his?"

"I appeal to you."

At that, he might have been cautious, for Anne Metlen was not one who appealed. She had laid a trap.

"How much do you want?"

"Twenty-five thousand dollars."

"Twenty-five thousand dollars." He repeated the phrase with the coldest sarcasm. "He's not man enough to ask for it, but you're woman enough to ask for it. What have you got left for collateral except that whorehouse across the tracks?"

She held out her hand, palm up, holding nothing. But what a hand it was. What an exquisite pattern of blue veins, what long, tapered fingers that might search and stroke. "You have my word."

"You're the collateral?"

The orchestra had packed their instruments and departed through the French doors.

"The bank can't loan you anything," he said. "But I'll give you a thousand dollars."

She smiled. She said, "A thousand dollars is not much to a man who is believed to be rich."

Then he smiled. "I'll give you a thousand dollars if you'll get up here on this table and take your clothes off."

She withdrew her hand. A drink was before her, and she drank it, and set down the glass, exactly where it had been. "Twenty-five thousand dollars."

Their eyes met. He paused.

She said, "Twenty-five thousand-dollar bills."

Thousand-dollar bills are now as rare as the dropping of the name, at a cocktail party, of the President whose likeness appears on them—Grover Cleveland. But once they were stylish among sports and touts acquainted with horses and with oil leases, who enjoyed flashing a bankroll. If the outer bill was for a thousand, these men, whatever their physical appearance or ignorance of the subjunctive mode, were welcomed almost everywhere even though the core of the big bill concealed was of fives and ones.

Twenty-five such bills, stacked, would fit snugly in her clutch purse.

Harry Connard was at once showing himself carelessly rich and tasting a revenge only the rich can afford and savor.

Those close enough to hear sat quiet before the unredeemed dishes of melted Neapolitan ice cream.

He got up. "I'll be right back."

Here was the opportunity for others to leave, but they did not, caught in a net suddenly so taut that to breathe was difficult, to light a cigarette impossible. There is no more passionate drive than that to humiliate. Because of her consent, Anne had already been humiliated. The bank was practically next door. How long does it take to walk a block, unlock a door, turn on a light, twirl a knob, move a steel door?

Had he been sober, Harry Connard might not have returned; then he might not have been shamed as badly as she. But she thought that he would return. So while she waited she thought about her husband and thanked God he was not in that town and prayed God he would not be in that town again.

And she silently asked, "Do you believe I love you, Zack?"

Connard returned.

She said, "Give me the money."

He did.

She counted it. She tucked it into her clutch purse, laid the purse on the table.

Agile as a cat, she stepped from a chair to the tabletop. She raised both arms, reached behind her; her fingers might have been sighted. With one motion she pulled the velvet sheath over her head and tossed it aside. She removed her chemise, and then with those sighted fingers she unhooked her brassiere and exposed the breasts her child sucked.

On another woman, a garter belt is an unappealing contrivance, necessary but unlovely, too reminiscent of drab device. Pavlova alone might have matched her shedding of it, and of her stockings and her shoes. It was choreography—a taut, brief episode—Offenbach, but in Dorian mode.

She turned once, slowly, paused, and turned back. She looked above their heads at the far wall, at the corner where false vines clung to the plumbing. And then she unclasped the choker of false pearls and tossed it; it struck a chair, and clattered to the floor like bones. She stood before them naked as Aphrodite, and as indifferent.

Some there present lived for many years; they seldom spoke of that evening. No one spoke now. In the past moments, they had observed what should not have been. One among them had required what is not to be required, and like all those who have debauched themselves, they crept away into the lobby of the Andrews Hotel, and from there into the dark.

The courthouse clock struck eleven; the shivering, gong-like tones drifted over the town and away.

*

Twelve hours later, Sunday morning, it struck again, a secular tone among the abusive clangings of the church bells, summoning those who believe in God and assume He appreciates their attention to Him—or those who were anxious to give God another chance to clear up some impossible mess. The church bells rang at eleven for good reason. Had they rung at ten, they would have brought into question Sunday as a day of rest when, for once, a man might roll over and go back to sleep; had they rung later than eleven, they would have interfered with the roast pork in the oven and the applesauce.

Just before those bells began to toll, two boys on bicycles met the train down from Butte. One was maybe twelve, the other fourteen—he was not so quick to smile. Both were professional in wearing around their pants leg, at the ankle, a clip to keep the chain from chewing up their clothes. After the baggage man threw off the big bundle of Sunday papers (he spoke to them by name), they knelt and cut the cords around the papers with pocket knives, stuffed the papers in heavy canvas bags, and rode away. They carried the bags ahead of them in wire baskets, and until some of the papers had been thrown at the front porches, they could hardly see over them. They were narrow-hipped, narrow-shouldered blond boys, maybe brothers. Their corduroys were worn but well washed, and their faces were clean; they were proper messengers of the news of the world. As the bells tolled, they rode up Pacific Street and down Rife. Mondays they delivered the *Grayling Examiner.* Wednesday, *The Saturday Evening Post.* Fridays they distributed fliers for the Rex Theater—one week the flyers might be red, another, green, another, yellow. Children liked the fliers. You could collect them, draw on them, fold them so they flew like aeroplanes.

Shortly before church was out, about the time the altar boy extinguished the candle on the Gospel side, the older boy delivered his last paper at the house of people named Boone. He approached the house carefully, because of the dog.

At noon the Boones, a middle-aged couple, returned from the Methodist Episcopal Church for their applesauce and roast pork simmering away in the oven of a new electric stove. The roast was tempting to the nose, and by now the heat of the new stove had certainly made harmless the worms that reside in pork.

The Boones were not at all in the social swim in Grayling, exactly why it was hard to say, for Boone himself was an officer in a small business and loan outfit, and Mrs. Boone was active in the church. She regularly attended Wednesday-night prayer meeting, and she went about collecting old clothes which she helped to stuff into barrels to send off to cover the naked, who, grateful, might turn to Jesus as Savior. A print of Holman Hunt's *The Light of the World* was prominent in the Boone living room, along with two delicately tinted glass-protected prints of obviously the same baby. The set was labeled "A Little Bit of Heaven" and below on one was printed AWAKE and on the other ASLEEP. But the Boones were quite childless, and kept an Airedale, a breed no longer much spoken of. The dog, Laddie, regarded almost everyone as dangerous to the Boones, to whom he owed everything. Even old friends made certain when calling at the Boone home to speak out their names clearly after ringing the doorbell so that the dog could be quieted and shut away from them. Sometimes people forgot, and simply walked in.

"You should have remembered," Mrs. Boone could only say. "You really should have remembered."

Now as she entered her house, she spoke again, the tail end of a longer speech. ". . . never able to show her face in town again."

Mr. Boone had been among those who had paused on the street when, every weekday, Anne Metlen drove past in the old Locomobile. He knew next to nothing about the present circumstances. "Well, I don't know about that," he said.

"Don't know about that? A woman naked—taking off her clothes and standing naked before dozens of people and some of them perfect strangers? And you don't know about that?"

"Maybe there were circumstances."

"Of course there were circumstances. She was drunk. How could she have been anything but drunk? Suppose I did such a thing?"

"Well, of course you wouldn't." That idea was appalling to him, but not for the reason she thought. It's a pity what gravity and starches and age make of the human body. After forty it is wise to keep well covered.

"Mark my words," Mrs. Boone said. "She'll not show her face in town again." It is pretty exciting to realize that there are people in the world who can never show their faces again. What are they going to do, these people, if they can't show their faces? Go to another town? But the past will catch up with them there. Kill themselves? The papers are full of things like that.

And it was a pity it was Sunday, a day on which Anne Metlen never appeared in the big old car, because the stores were closed, but anybody might imagine what she was feeling. Most certainly she would pull down the shades against those who might drive by her own house on some pretended errand, longing to see the face of a woman who could never show her face again.

Oh, how Sunday did drag on.

The Sunday newspaper down from Butte was not much help. Two gambling houses and five "houses of prostitution" had been raided and closed. But men would go right on gambling across the street, and the whores would go right on working, though on another street. Mercury Street might lie fallow for a year. Butte was fun.

The name of this man Harding was mentioned.

GERMANY MUST BE FORCED TO PAY, SAYS SOLON. But pay with what? In that very paper was published a picture of an old man with a wheelbarrow piled high with paper German marks he was about to exchange for a loaf of bread. But Butte was sixty miles away, and Germany even farther.

What was so shocking about a woman's being nude in public? Would it be so awful if a man did that? Was the town so strange today because she had exposed that secret opening that received the seed of human life—human life whose purpose has never been well explained, and which for everybody ends in agony and death? It's a heavy one, the responsibility for creating a human life.

But that Sunday—why, it felt as if there had been an important death, a death that closes shops and stores for half a day and little children stand silent a moment in the classroom.

Monday was not much better. The new sprinkling truck left the City Garage at five that morning to settle the dust; the spray gave a little hope to small, expiring grass at the curb.

The girls in the Red-White-and-Blue Rooms slept exhausted after an active weekend. What do you suppose they made of what had happened?

At six, the colored man, Brown, began swabbing the white tiles in the lobby of the Andrews Hotel. The night people had called it a day—a cook at the Sugar Bowl Café, the watchman at the normal school, and the telegraph operator in the Union Pacific depot. Into his office, behind the window barred with brass rods and just enough room below to shove a hand with a ticket or a telegram, he invited certain people in the dead of night for strong black coffee brewed over a Sterno stove. His early life he had spent in Peru, and he spoke fluent Spanish to this day. Among his visitors from time to time was a high school boy who was taught Spanish by Miss Schoenborn, herself no more Spanish than her sensible Cuban heels.

Oh how that boy did wish he had grown up in Peru, and that so much else, so much else were different for him that didn't bear speaking of. The lady all this had happened to had once smiled at him on the street, from her car. Only that—and suddenly he had wings.

Many little things are known about attractive people; others have made it their business to find out. They know where and of what material attractive people choose their dresses, what they wish to see set before them in a restaurant, and what books they read. What you know of attractive people makes them a little bit yours, for they shape your dreams, sometimes, and alter your style. In fact, were it not for them, you wouldn't be you.

It was known of Anne Metlen that on Monday mornings just past nine, she drove the Locomobile down Rife Street around the corner to Pacific Street, and the street changed, and for a few moments Grayling was a city apart.

Now again it was Monday morning, and eight forty-five.

On Pacific Street little groups waited, not quite conspicuous. Four people stood near the revolving door of the Andrews Hotel, and a few men stood near the green baggage cart at the depot, leaning forward on their elbows.

What they knew was at second hand—the men who had been present in the dining room of the Andrews Hotel were not among them; perhaps each was afraid to meet the eyes of another who had remained present when he might have left, and was now marked for having witnessed what he should not have witnessed. Baptist, Episcopalian or Catholic he might be—prompt to repay a debt and patient with little children—but in his bowels he knew that for such sacrilege the old gods struck a man blind.

The courthouse clock had already tolled nine.

In a few minutes the watchers began to move off. She had of course claimed her last advantage—to keep out of sight. That's what anybody would do. It was only that they had hoped for something beyond. An example. As for them, things would be as they were; the hours would move as ever and someday end, and there was no magic anywhere.

Only the high school boy expected otherwise. Maybe he hadn't yet known humiliation and the need to hide his face. Maybe. But he had put his future into her hands—that was the least he could do. Even as the others had drifted away, his eyes remained fixed on a spot far up Pacific Street, the sun at his back. In the wintertime the sun rose just behind the grain elevator; now in the summertime it rose behind the old Metlen Hotel, a little north or south. The sun was so high now you couldn't guess just where it rose.

But at seven past nine it struck hard on the windshield of an automobile turning from Rife to Pacific Street.

*

Warren G. Harding was elected that November by a nation sick of the war and sick of Europe. Americans were anxious to get back to the business of business. Harding looked every inch a President. His acceptance speech was broadcast—a historic broadcast made possible in part by a circuit designed and patented by Zachary Metlen. His wife did not hear that broadcast. She and her little boy, John, had already sailed for France.